Night of the VANISHING LIGHTS

Lee Roddy

PUBLISHING

Colorado Springs, Colorado

NIGHT OF THE VANISHING LIGHTS
Copyright © 1994 by Lee Roddy

Library of Congress Cataloging-in-Publication Data
Roddy, Lee, 1921-
    Night of the vanishing lights / Lee Roddy
        p.   cm. — (Ladd family adventure : 10)
    Summary: Josh and his friends investigate mysterious lights on Molokai and
try to figure out how to get a valuable surfboard back from the neighborhood bully,
Kong.
    ISBN 1-56179-256-X
    [1. Hawaii—Fiction.   2.   Mystery and detective stories.]
I. Title.   II. Series: Roddy, Lee, 1921-   Ladd family adventure : 10.
PZ7.R6N1   1994
[Fic]—dc20

                                                         94-15779
                                                           CIP
                                                              AC

Published by Focus on the Family Publishing, Colorado Springs, Colorado 80903.
Distributed by Word Books, Dallas, Texas.

Editor: Ron Klug
Cover Illustration: Paul Casale
Cover Design: James Lebbad

Printed in the United States of America

94 95 96 97 98 99 / 10 9 8 7 6 5 4 3 2 1

*To Mrs. Lee Hicks
and her third-grade classes
at Forest Lake Christian School,
Auburn, California,
in appreciation of their annual
Lee Roddy Book Report Month*

CONTENTS

Chapter One

THE NIGHT WALKERS

Josh Ladd was the first to see the mysterious lights, but he thought nothing of them until he realized that Victor Aka* had seen them too. The island-born boy broke off his singing, staring openmouthed toward the mountain. Then he leaped to his feet, accidentally kicking sand over Josh and his best friend, Tank Catlett, who still sat on the beach.

"What's the matter?" Josh asked in sudden alarm.

"Yeah, Victor," Tank added in his slow, easy manner from where he sat before the dying campfire. "You look scared to death."

"It's them!" thirteen-year-old Victor answered in a dry croak.

"Who are *them*— I mean, who are *they*?" Josh asked, standing barefooted and brushing the seat of his cutoff blue jeans.

"The night walkers!" Victor's voice was a hoarse whisper. He stood with his back to the channel separating the Island of Molokai* from the Island of Maui.* He faced inland where the nearly 5,000 foot high Kamakou* peak in the Molokai Forest rose into the night sky. The flickering lights, like flaming torches, were clearly visible through the trees on the mountainside.

Victor kept his eyes on the strange lights but reached both brown hands down to snatch up his ukulele* and bamboo beach mat. "Come on! Let's get out of here!"

"Why?" Josh asked, studying the lights. They were spaced out, one behind the other, as though some marchers in single file with flaming torches were winding their way down the mountainside toward the ocean. "You told us they were legendary, like the menehunes.*"

Victor's voice rose to a frightened squeak. "No! I said they're supposed to be, and I'd never seen any. Until now." He started across the beach toward the rural road. "Are you two coming, or not?"

Josh raised his eyebrows as a question to Tank. He hesitated, and Josh was sure he was thinking the same thing. Between songs around the campfire that evening, Victor had told many Hawaiian legends and beliefs that he had learned from his parents and grandparents. That included the strange night walkers, mysterious little people who lived high up in the hills.

During hoku,* the full moon, Victor had solemnly declared, the night walkers take their spears and walk down to fish in the ocean. If someone built a house or otherwise put an obstruction in the path the night walkers took, they would walk right through it.

"Coming?" Victor repeated anxiously, again heading toward the road.

Josh didn't answer, but asked Tank, "You scared?"

"Of what?" Tank asked indignantly. "There are no such things as night walkers or menehunes."

"That's what I say," Josh answered, watching Victor disappear into the night. "So that means those lights have to be from something else. Let's check them out."

"Uh . . . " Tank's voice suggested a sudden change of mind. "I thought you just wanted to know if I was scared?"

"I did, and since you're not, let's investigate to find out what's really going on with those torches."

Tank hesitated. "We've never been on this island before, so we could get lost."

"How can we do that? We can see the reflection of the water behind us, so we know that's south. The mountains straight ahead are north. West is to our left and east to the right. So let's move."

Tank groaned softly as Josh raised his voice to Victor. "We're going to see who's really carrying those lights."

"You'll be sorry!" Victor called back from the roadway. It was dark and deserted, like much of rural Molokai. It is one of the smallest islands in the Hawaiian chain, and about the least touched by tourist trade. Molokai is largely inhabited by kamaainas,* or native-born residents. "See you back at the house—I hope."

"Cheery thought, huh, Tank?" Josh asked. Without waiting for an answer, Josh hurriedly picked up his beach mat and towel. It didn't occur to him that Tank was a reluctant participant in many of their hair-raising adventures. Josh did know that where he led, Tank followed, so Josh was always careful to avoid trouble. However, it sometimes seemed to come looking for him.

The two boys hurriedly buried their dying campfire with sand, then slipped on their tennis shoes without socks. Shirtless and wearing only cutoffs, they hurried over the beach and crossed the deserted road. Victor was nowhere in sight. Josh and Tank headed toward the mountain rising massive and threatening above them.

"Who do you suppose is really carrying those lights?" Tank asked as the darkness closed in around them.

"Probably some local islanders, but I can't guess why." Josh wished he had brought a flashlight as they left the palm trees behind and came to a dense stand of trees he couldn't identify in the night.

He began to puff slightly as he reached the base of the mountain. He kept the mysterious torches in sight while mentally reviewing what Victor had said about the night walkers.

They were taller than Hawaii's mythical menehunes, who worked only at night, building roads or fish ponds. If the work wasn't completed before dawn, the menehunes left the work forever unfinished. Night walkers, as Victor had explained, were more elusive, being known only by their lights. No local island boy had ever dared get close to them for fear that the night walkers might go right through them.

"Hey! I just thought of something," Josh exclaimed. "Victor said they only come down when the moon is full, and there's certainly no full moon tonight."

"Maybe whoever's carrying those lights doesn't have a calendar," Tank replied.

Josh started to chuckle at his friend's humor, but stopped just as the pale moon topped the mountain peak to the boys' right. The lights suddenly vanished.

"Hey!" Tank exclaimed. "Where'd they go?"

The boys stopped, staring up at the mountain. "I don't know," Josh admitted. "They just . . . " he broke off his thought and grabbed Tank's bare arm. "Look!" Josh whispered. "There's something over there behind that tree. I saw it move."

Both boys stood still, trying to control their noisy breathing while their eyes probed the deeper shadows. The moon made every leaf and branch seem alive with threats of danger.

From the direction of the tree, a voice quavered in spooky tones: "Stop! Turn back!"

Josh heard Tank gasp as the voice continued, rising and falling in a ghostly manner. "Turn back before it's too laaaate!"

Tank whispered, "Let's get out of here."

"Wait!" Josh answered, his voice low. "That's just somebody trying to scare us off."

"Well, they're succeeding!"

Josh raised his voice and called toward the voice. "Look, whoever you are, we aren't doing anything wrong, and this is public property, so..."

"This is kapu* place!" the trembly voice interrupted. "Leave before you bring on the revenge of the night walkers." The last two words seemed to vibrate in the darkness before fading away like a dying echo.

Tank tugged at Josh's arm. "Let's go!"

Josh stood his ground. "We don't believe in..."

Whoosh! Something whizzed between Josh's and Tank's heads, making them duck instinctively. Something thudded into a tree trunk behind them and vibrated there, like an arrow or a spear from a skindiver's sling gun.* Josh had heard one some time ago when a fisherman had accidentally discharged one in Josh's direction.

"The next one will not miss," the scary voice warned.

"I'm convinced!" Tank exclaimed, turning to start stumbling down the mountain.

The phantom voice's last threat sent a shudder through twelve-year-old Josh. He was adventuresome but not foolish. "Wait for me!" he called, and with a pounding heart, raced after his friend.

Behind him the ghostlike voice broke into weird, maniacal laughter.

In their haste, the boys stumbled wildly down the mountain,

dodging trees and brush and trying not to trip over vines and tree roots. Josh kept his bearings by watching for the moonlight to reflect off the water at the edge of the mountain. The road, which ran along the south shore, would lead them to where Victor lived.

Panting hard, Josh and Tank started to plunge between some shadowy trees, but the first sharp thorns that brushed against Josh's bare legs made him stop.

"Ouch! Kiawe trees!* Can't go that way!" He looked quickly to right and left. "This way," he said, moving to his left. "I think we can go around them over there."

They found an opening in the thorny kiawe and scrambled over rough volcanic rock that had been deposited there ages before. They had gone only a few feet when a dark hulking wall loomed before them.

"Now what?" Tank asked, stopping with Josh to look up at the obstruction. It was about three feet higher than the boys' heads.

"We can feel our way around," Josh replied, reaching to touch the rough lava rocks. "Hey! You know what this must be?"

"Does it matter? Let's get around . . . "

"It's a heiau,* a platform used for religious ceremonies by ancient Hawaiians! They're flat on top, you know, so if we can crawl up, we can make good time without getting all scratched up with those thorns."

Feeling their way, the boys found hand- and footholds in the crevices of the volcanic rocks. These had been laid by hand centuries before and had partly crumbled by neglect. In a few moments, with bleeding fingers and scratched knees, the boys stood upright on the heiau.

In the weak moonlight, the platform stretched out as flat as a tabletop for about a hundred feet in all directions.

"Let's not just stand here," Tank urged. "That thing might be right behind us."

Josh hesitated, glancing quickly in all directions. "I'm getting my bearings. There, that's the ocean! See it just beyond those trees?"

"I'm looking behind us, hoping not to see or hear whoever or whatever warned us off back there."

"You'd better look where we're going," Josh warned. "We should be on the road in just a few minutes."

They dashed across the heiau, their tennis shoes taking severe cuts and scratches from the rough volcanic rocks. At the far end, they stopped for breath and to make sure nothing or nobody was following them. The heiau was cold and still. With a grateful sigh, the boys eased over the side and picked their way through trees and brush toward the sea.

When they reached the roadway, they started laughing with relief. After a few minutes of jogging, they saw Victor's house. He and his mother were standing on the small open lanai* under bright electric lights.

"What happened to you guys?" Victor demanded. He was short and stocky with olive skin, dark hair, and brown eyes still wide with fright.

"That's what I want to know," his mother assured them. She was a striking woman about six feet tall with pale brown skin, dark eyes, and shoulder-length black hair tinged with traces of gray. "Victor told me some wild tale about you two trying to see the night walkers up close. Is that true?"

"We tried," Josh admitted, using a tanned hand to wipe perspiration from his forehead and to brush back his damp, wavy brown hair from his blue eyes.

"Yeah!" Tank agreed, still so excited he almost rushed his words. "But we ran into something . . . "

"Some*one*," Josh corrected.

"Come into the kitchen," Mrs. Aka said, opening the screen door. "Get some cold drinks and tell us all about it."

Josh had nearly drained his can of soda when he and Tank finished retelling their adventure, seated around the breakfast nook, their drinks on the small tabletop.

Victor's mother had kept shaking her head all during the retelling. "I can understand somebody trying to frighten you boys off by using a scary voice, but I can't imagine anyone shooting a spear gun at you. I'd better call the police."

As she stood, the yellow wall phone hanging by the sink rang sharply. All three boys jumped and looked at the instrument as Mrs. Aka picked it up. She listened a moment, then looked at Josh.

"Yes, Mrs. Ladd, he and Tank are right here."

Josh rose and took the receiver from the hostess. "Hi, Mom," he said into the phone.

"Hello, Josh," she said over the wire from their apartment in Honolulu.* "Guess who just called from the Mainland?"

"Oh, Mom, don't make me guess again." He really didn't care, and he had long ago given up trying to figure out which of their old friends would next phone from California. They always said the same thing: they were heading for Hawaii, and wouldn't it be fun to get together again? Even people the Ladds had barely known in Los Angeles did that.

It really meant the visitors expected to be met at the airport, driven around to all the sights, taken to dinner, and perhaps invited to be house guests.

Josh's disinterested mind had drifted so that when his mother spoke again, he almost didn't hear the name.

Then he jumped as though touched by an electric wire. "Who did you say, Mom?" he asked in disbelief.

"Daniel Davis. You remember . . . "

"Disaster Davis?" Josh interrupted, almost yelling into the receiver.

Tank leaped up from the table and stood, rigid as a telephone pole. His face, usually a golden tan, was as white as his straight hair, which the Hawaiian sun had bleached from blond. "Diz Davis? What about him?"

"He's coming to visit us for a week. Talk to you later, Mom."

Tank slapped his forehead with an open palm. "Oh, no! Not him!"

Josh nodded. "First the night walkers, and now Disaster Davis! We're headed for monstrous problems!"

Chapter Two

QUESTIONS FROM A STRANGER

Two days later, Josh and Tank were standing outside their apartment building in Honolulu talking to another friend about both their experience on Molokai and Disaster Davis coming to visit.

Josh concluded, "I have to get back over to Molokai and find out more about those strange lights. I don't want to do it while Diz is here, but he won't go home until after the next full moon."

"He'll be here seven days, hmm?" Manuel Souza murmured thoughtfully. At thirteen, he was a year older than Josh and Tank, and considered to be very smart, very akamai,* and probably the top student in school. He was olive-skinned with dark, wavy hair and deep brown eyes. He wore faded bathing trunks that once had been green.

He lived with his widowed mother in a small house down the street from the three-story apartment building where Josh and Tank resided.

When Manuel continued his silent contemplation, Josh asked, "What are you thinking?"

Manuel replied, "You say that Victor claims the night walkers come down the mountain only during the full moon. Is that right?"

"That's what he said," Josh agreed. "But I reminded Tank that when we saw the lights, the moon wasn't full. So I'm sure that there are no so-called night walkers on that island."

"But," Tank said, "if you're right, who or what made those lights we saw? And why?" Tank's nose was always sunburned, usually red and flaking, but now it was covered with a white salve.

"I don't know," Josh admitted, "but that's why I want to get back over there and find out."

Manuel said, "Since you're convinced the lights were man-made, then there's a possibility that whoever caused them doesn't want anybody to go poking around, trying to find out about them. It could be dangerous."

"I wish you hadn't said that," Tank complained. "That will just make Josh more curious than ever, and he'll end up in trouble. What's worse, I'll probably be with him, as usual, and I'll be in trouble too."

"I don't think it's really going to be dangerous," Josh replied.

The three boys turned toward the apartment building when Roger Okamoto called out and hurried to join them.

He was thirteen, very slender, with copper-colored skin and intensely black hair that stuck out above his ears. He wore his usual faded blue cutoffs with sandals but no shirt.

"What you bruddahs* talk, yeah?" he asked in pidgin English,* his voice going up at the end. He normally spoke proper English, but often reverted to the language spoken by many of Hawaii's diverse multicultural groups.

As Josh and Tank explained, Roger's almond-shaped eyes opened wide. Like many islanders, he believed that most of Hawaii's many legends were true, although he vigorously denied that he was superstitious.

"Don't mess with da kine* night walkers," he solemnly warned.

"There aren't any such things," Josh replied.

"I think there are," Roger replied, switching to proper English. "I don't like to talk about such things."

Manuel suggested, "Tell Roger about your friend who's coming to visit. What'd you call him? Disaster Davis?"

"Diz for short," Tank explained.

Roger asked, "Why do you call him that?"

"Because that's what he is," Tank replied. "Diz is a walking, talking disaster that can happen anywhere, anytime. Like the time when Josh and I tried out for the school band, where Diz played the tuba. Remember, Josh?"

He replied sadly, "Oh, yes. I remember."

Tank continued, "When he saw Josh and me walk in, he got so excited he yelled, 'All *right*!' leaped up and tripped over the music stand. He fell headfirst with the tuba right through the big bass drum."

Manuel laughed. "You're kidding."

"I wish I were," Tank replied solemnly.

Manuel asked, "But how did that get you boys in trouble?"

"That didn't," Tank admitted, "but he usually does. Like the time . . . "

"Hold on, Tank," Josh interrupted. "We don't want to give Roger and Manuel the wrong idea about Diz. He's really a nice guy who tries very hard to do the right things. But he's all arms and legs, and they aren't coordinated, and sometimes he doesn't think things through too well."

"Yeah," Tank agreed. "Like the time our school had a pet show, but Diz didn't have a dog or cat or anything. So he went to a man who sells skunks. The dealer assured Diz that all the skunks except one had their scent glands removed, and so those were safe." He added quickly, "I can tell that you already know what happened, right?"

"Sure!" Roger replied. "Diz accidentally got the one that still had its scent glands."

"It was an easy mistake," Josh defended Diz. "The skunk was a gentle, friendly animal and didn't cause any trouble for the day Diz had him before the pet show."

"That year both Josh and I had dogs, which we had entered in the show," Tank concluded quickly. "On the morning it was to start, Josh and I arrived late with our dogs. They took one look at that skunk and charged."

Josh and Tank joined Roger and Manuel in laughing, although Josh still felt terrible about the pet show suddenly being cancelled and people still blaming them. As Manuel and Roger wiped tears of laughter from their eyes, the four boys started strolling down the cul-de-sac* street.

Josh said, "Maybe you two can come up with some idea of how Tank and I can get back to Molokai and find out the truth about those night walker lights, but without taking Diz along. There's no telling what he might do."

Roger suggested, "Why don't you take him with you to the heiau and leave him there? You could slip off by yourselves and investigate the lights, then come back for Diz later."

Tank shook his head. "How could we do that?"

"Well," Roger replied, "there's that old snipe hunting* trick."

"Yeah!" Tank agreed enthusiastically. "We could give him a sack and tell him to hold it open and make a certain kind of noise to call the snipe."

"Tell him it's a Hawaiian snipe," Roger suggested.

"Right!" Tank continued. "We'd tell him that Josh and I were going off to drive the birds toward Diz. He mustn't move, but wait until we come back. Yeah! I like it!"

Josh shook his head. "How would you guys like it if someone did that to you?"

Tank protested, "Oh, Josh, Diz couldn't get hurt."

"I just don't feel right about it," Josh replied.

"It could help make up for the messes he's gotten us into . . . ," Tank began, then broke off in mid-sentence. He stared at the big boy stepping through the oleanders* and be-still* trees that lined the eastern side of the street. He wore old khaki-colored cutoffs and carried a short surfboard under his massive left arm.

"King Kong!" Tank exclaimed in a low voice.

"We're safe with so many of us," Manuel said quickly.

Josh heard Tank gulp at the sight of the neighborhood bully. His real name was Kamuela* Kong, but the nickname nobody ever used to his face was because of his size and appearance, which resembled the movie monster gorilla of the 1930s. Kong was big; there was no doubt of that. Barely thirteen, he stood six feet tall and weighed around 200 pounds. He had wide, flaring nostrils, curly black hair, and deep brown eyes.

His disposition was even, everyone agreed—always mad and looking for some luckless boy to punch out. Before he did that, he terrorized his victim by slowly pulling black leather gloves over hands the size of unhusked coconuts.

Now strutting toward the boys, he reminded Josh of a tall fire hydrant with legs. Kong's bare feet were immense. Nobody had ever seen Kong wearing shoes, not even at Christmas. Once, in a rare moment when he was not trying to pound on Josh, Kong had proudly told him that he had at one time had his feet measured in a shoe store. He would have needed a size thirteen, triple E in a man's size.

Kong always spoke in pidgin English. He called, "Hey, you guys! Want go surfing?" His voice rose at the end, leaving the final word hanging in the air.

Surprised at not getting beat up or chased, the boys looked at each other and promptly made truthful excuses. Josh and Tank had no boards. Roger's had a broken skeg,* and Manuel's mother had confiscated his for breaking a house rule.

"Too bad," Kong replied somberly, then added brightly, "but no problem, yeah? We all walk to dah beach anyhow."

The boys reluctantly agreed, anxious to avoid setting up a situation in which Kong might feel he had cause to seek them out individually and thump on them.

Uneasily walking west toward famous Waikiki Beach,* Josh kept trying to figure out why Kong wasn't being his usual nasty self. Finally, Kong told them.

"Da kine makauhine,* she planty huhu* foh* me."

It took Josh a moment to translate for himself: Kong's mother was very angry with him. He had never seen Mrs. Kong, but Roger and Manuel had. They said she was a widow who stood six-foot, six-inches tall, weighed more than 300 pounds, and was the only person in the world of whom Kamuela was afraid.

Josh, Tank, Roger, and Manuel cautiously expressed sympathy.

Kong brightened. "You guys understand da kine mad mama," he said, lowering his voice to a confidential level. "She huhu my bes' friend, Komo. Say I can't talk wit' him foh whan week!" He held up a brown finger the size of an overgrown sausage. "Long time! Den, aftah that, she say she send me to Molokai foh live few days with cal-abash cousin.* But moh bettah* dat way, yeah?"

Again, the boys indicated careful agreement.

Josh remembered that Diz was coming and asked Kong, "When are you going to be on Molokai?"

Kong shrugged. "Don't know yet. Soon."

Josh and Tank exchanged anxious glances. Disaster Davis would arrive tomorrow, which meant it was almost certain that he and Kong would meet here in Honolulu. The thought was enough to give Josh shivers. He fervently hoped that nothing would happen to make Kong mad again, but, knowing Diz, Josh wasn't going to count on that. On the other hand, Kong's schedule also meant he would be on Molokai at the same time Josh and Tank would return, hopefully without Disaster Davis. Either way, keeping Kong and Diz apart would be a major challenge.

Tank seemed to read Josh's mind, for he rolled his eyes skyward and drew his forefinger across his throat.

"Good!" Kong beamed at them. "Today, we holo holo* dah beach. You guys watch. Kong teach you surf good. You bruddahs planty lucky Kong do dat foh you, yeah?"

The boys tried to make sounds that seemed to agree, but without actually committing themselves.

"Hey!" Kong added, reaching out huge arms to drape them casu-ally like fallen palm trees across Roger's and Manuel's shoulders, "let's all go Molokai togethah!"

The boys promptly expressed regrets, making various excuses.

Later, sitting morosely on the beach watching Kong show off on moderate sets of waves, Tank moaned as though in pain. "I think I liked it better when Kong wasn't our friend. At least we didn't know where he was going to be, or when. Now we have all this misery to look forward to."

"Diz will be here tomorrow," Josh said thoughtfully. "How are we going to keep him and Kong apart?"

"I don't know," Manuel replied, "but I'm going to see if my parents will send me to the Big Island until your friend Diz goes home."

"Me, too," Roger agreed solemnly.

"Thanks," Tank replied sarcastically. "You guys are a big comfort."

"At least we'll be alive next week," Roger answered with a cheerful grin. "I'm not sure about you two."

"Our only hope," Tank said in his slow, thoughtful manner, "is to keep Diz and Kong from meeting. But how?"

The boys watched Kong showing off on his surfboard, but their conversations were entirely focused on various ways to keep Kong and Diz apart. When Kong rode the last wave in and waded ashore toward them, they had not come up with a single workable idea.

Back at the apartments, when Kong had taken his surfboard and ducked through the oleanders, Josh, Tank, Roger, and Manuel stood under the Ladds' carport.

"Maybe he's changing," Josh said hopefully.

"I don't think so," Tank said, staring at the place where Kong had gone. "He'll soon be meaner than ever."

The sliding screen door on the Ladds' second-floor lanai slid open, and Josh's mother called out, "Josh, are you down there?"

"Yes." He stepped out to where she could see him.

"Telephone. Your friend from Molokai is calling. Says it's important."

Josh took the outside stairs two at a time, left his shoes outside the apartment door, and ran barefooted across the rattan rug to the phone. "Hi, Victor. What's up?"

"I don't know, but I thought you and Tank should know about it."

Josh frowned. "About what?"

"Some kids I know said a stranger had stopped them walking home from school and asked if they knew where two haole* boys lived, and they described you and Tank."

Josh's insides tightened, remembering the scary-voiced thing he and Tank had encountered on the mountainside. "Did this stranger have a funny voice?"

"My friends didn't say. But he's a haole, and there aren't many on his side of Molokai, so they told the stranger about you and Tank visiting me."

Josh felt a strong sense of uneasiness. "Did he come to see you?"

"No, maybe because my friends knew where you and Tank lived, so they told this guy."

"They told him where we live?"

"Sure. They didn't see any harm in it, and neither do I. But I thought you should know about it anyway."

Josh and Victor talked a moment longer, then ended with Josh reminding him that they would pick up Diz Davis at the airport tomorrow. "Will it be okay with you for me to bring Diz along?"

"Sure."

After Josh hung up the phone, he walked out on the lanai and stared thoughtfully down to the entrance to the cul-de-sac leading to the apartments. He half expected to see a stranger driving slowly up the street.

It doesn't make any sense, Josh told himself. *If he's the same guy Tank and I heard on Molokai, why should he want to know where we live? We didn't do anything except try to investigate some lights. We didn't even get a look at him, just heard his voice. But I guess he saw us enough to know we're haoles, and then to ask questions of the locals.*

Josh shuddered, remembering the sound of the spear gun that had been fired just before he and Tank ran.

Suddenly Josh wasn't sure that having Disaster Davis visit was the worst thing that could happen in the next few days.

Chapter Three

A DISASTROUS MEETING

Josh's father drove Josh and Tank to the sprawling Honolulu Airport to meet Diz's plane. John Ladd was a former high school history teacher who now owned a tourist publication in Waikiki.* He was six feet tall, with clean-cut features and dark wavy hair.

He parked the family station wagon in one of the lots, bought Josh a fragrant yellow-white plumeria* lei* and Tank a vanda* orchid one so that they each might present one to the new arrival in keeping with island traditions.

Josh was apprehensive as he slipped his lei across his left forearm to carry the delicate blossoms without crushing them. The lei still dripped slightly from the water that kept it fresh.

"That must be his plane," Tank said, pointing out to sea off of Diamond Head.*

"Made it this far," Josh mumbled, watching the huge jumbo jet as it swept low over the blue-green water offshore, then made a ninety-degree turn and settled onto the long runway.

"Down safely," Josh said quietly.

Tank lowered his voice so Mr. Ladd couldn't hear and cautioned,

"Don't relax yet."

It was terrible, Josh decided, knowing there was this really nice guy who seemed to attract sudden disasters. Having Diz as a guest for seven whole days was going to be a nerve-wracking experience.

The trade winds, soft and gentle and warm, tousled Josh's dark wavy hair as he entered the open-air terminal flanked by his father and Tank.

At last the plane was parked at the gate and passengers began streaming down into the concourse.

"There he is," Tank said, pointing.

Josh had an impression of a child's stick-figure drawing, because Disaster Davis was very tall and thin, mostly arms and legs. His head appeared too big for the long, skinny neck.

Mr. Ladd observed, "He's grown since I last saw him. He's taller than both of you by half a head."

"Yeah," Tank whispered, leaning close to Josh. "That's what he's got, too—half a head."

Josh jabbed Tank in the ribs, then watched as the shy boy with the sandy hair and freckled face caught sight of them. He waved, smiled, hitched the garment bag over his shoulder, and started running toward them.

"Look out!" Josh cried, but it was too late.

Diz's garment bag swung into a portly woman walking beside him. Off balance, she started to fall. Josh and Tank groaned together as Diz turned to grab her. The garment bag slipped off his shoulder and landed on top of the lady, knocking her sprawling. She landed in a most undignified manner on her considerable backside.

"Oh, no! Not already!" Tank groaned as Diz reached down toward the woman. She clutched her purse as though she thought the boy was trying to snatch it. Then she sat up and began beating him with it.

Josh, his father, and Tank mercifully were too far away to hear what was being said as fellow passengers and uniformed airline personnel surrounded the woman and Diz. Josh couldn't see any more, for which he was glad.

Tank turned to Josh and said in a low, awed voice, "I know these islands were made by volcanoes, and they've stood for thousands of years. I just hope they can last through Diz's visit."

"I just hope it doesn't get any worse," Josh said.

Tank lowered his voice so Mr. Ladd couldn't hear. "Maybe we should take Diz to Molokai and let the night walkers have a shot at him." Tank paused, then added, "If we all live long enough to get back to Molokai."

When everything settled down, Mr. Ladd herded the boys into the old white station wagon and drove back to the apartment.

Diz, in wide-eyed wonder, kept fingering the two leis about his neck. "I never smelled anything so good," he said, sniffing the plumeria garland for the umpteenth time. "And I never saw an orchid outside a florist's shop. Now I have a whole herd of them around my neck. Oh, Josh and Tank, you are the best friends I ever had, doing all this for me."

Josh felt a little guilty because of his secret thoughts, but a glance at Tank showed his eyes bright with anticipation. Josh knew that his best friend was looking forward to getting even with Diz for all the trouble he had gotten them into—with the promise of more to come in the next few days.

Diz, sitting between Josh and Tank, reached long, thin arms over the backseat and settled one hand on each of their shoulders. "Just like old times, huh, guys? The three of us having fun. Hey, you know what I want to do first?"

Josh was afraid to ask, but he had no choice. "What?" he asked a little fearfully.

"Go surfing at Waikiki Beach!* You guys ever been there?"

"Many times," Tank assured him. "We live about a mile away."

Josh commented, "I don't remember you surfing, Diz."

"I don't, but I'll learn fast. Let's go tomorrow."

"Neither of us has a surfboard," Josh explained.

Diz replied hopefully, "Maybe we can borrow one."

"Not many guys will loan their boards," Josh said.

Diz shrugged. "Well, it was a good idea."

Josh was grateful that nothing happened the rest of the day and that night. He and Tank introduced Diz to Manuel and Roger, while Josh hoped that King Kong didn't show up. Diz's shy manner and wide-eyed innocence won Manuel and Roger over.

They agreed to go along to Waikiki Beach in the morning. Roger and Manuel also agreed that they would just take their swim fins and masks. That way, they could snorkel and show Diz the hidden beauty of Hawaii that was under water.

The next morning, with Josh still half asleep because Diz had excitedly talked much of the night, the five boys met downstairs by the Ladd carport beside the cul-de-sac.

As the five boys started walking down the street, Diz spotted two surfboards sticking up over the railing on the ground-floor lanai of the second building they were passing. One was much longer than the other.

"Hey, you guys!" he exclaimed. "There are a couple of surfboards. Maybe we could borrow them."

"Wait!" Josh called, but Diz was already moving like a broken windmill, arms and legs flailing, toward the front door beside the lanai.

Roger hissed, "You know who lives there? Old Man Blackheart, the only man I know who's as mean as King Kong! But I didn't know he had any surfboards."

The door opened promptly, but instead of the nasty-tempered bachelor the boys expected, a girl of about twelve stood there in a bright red muumuu* adorned with yellow blossoms.

"Wonder who she is?" Tank asked under his breath.

She was tiny, not even five feet tall, with shiny black shoulder-length hair cut in bangs over her forehead.

Josh noticed that Diz had suddenly become flustered and tongue-tied. Josh nudged the other boys and grinned. "You'd think Diz had never spoken to a girl before," he said.

"Not one like dat!" Roger said in pidgin, his voice taking on an awed tone. "She one nani wahine.*"

Josh glanced at Roger in surprise, for he had never been known to show any interest in any girl, and certainly had never said anything about one being pretty.

"She's not bad," Tank admitted. "What kind of Hawaiian mixture do you think she is, Josh?"

He studied the girl with the pale brown skin, tiny upturned nose, and delicate face that was almost doll-like. He took pride in being able to tell the difference between Hawaii's multicultural population by observing the small, unique characteristics of the various races.

"Cosmopolitan," he guessed. "Hapahaole,* some Hawaiian and Chinese."

The girl turned to the four boys and gave them a pleasant smile. "Your friend is having trouble expressing himself," she explained in precise English.

Tank gave Josh a gentle shove. "Go tell her."

"Okay, but all of you come with me."

As the four friends approached, Josh saw that the girl was unlike any other in the two apartment buildings on this street.

Diz retreated, his face bright red. "I stammered," he confessed. "I never did that before in my life. Josh, you tell her about the surfboard."

"Hi," Josh began, staring at the girl in the doorway. "I'm Josh Ladd. He's Diz . . . uh . . . Daniel Davis. And they are Tank Catlett, Roger Okamoto, and Manuel Souza. We all live on this street, except for . . . Daniel. He just got in from the Mainland yesterday."

"I'm Kalani Gilhooley," she said in a surprisingly musical voice.

"Gilhooley?" Tank exclaimed. "You're Irish?"

"My father is." She turned her warm smile on Tank. "My mother is Hawaiian and Chinese. We just moved in, but my father's on the Mainland. He'll be here in a few days, so we're all going to be neighbors."

"What happened to the man who lived here?" Manuel asked.

"I don't know," the girl replied. "I guess he moved out. Anyway, Mom and I arrived late last night from Haleiwa,* and you're the first neighbors I've met." She turned back to Josh. "Now, what was your friend Daniel trying to say?"

"We're all going down to Waikiki Beach. It'll be the first time he's ever seen it, so he wanted to borrow one of your surfboards."

The girl's smiled slowly faded, and she hesitated.

Josh thought, *Of course she's not going to loan it. She's just trying to think of a good excuse. That suits me, because I'm afraid Diz will let something happen to it.*

"I . . . ," Kalani began uncertainly. "One board is mine. The other belongs to my father. I know he wouldn't loan his."

"That's okay," Josh assured her, feeling relieved. "We understand."

A woman's voice called from inside the apartment. "Kalani, I need your help right now!"

"My mom," the girl explained. "We're unpacking, so I answered the doorbell." She hesitated, then added, "But since we're going to be neighbors, I'll loan you my board if you'll promise to bring it back this afternoon."

"We promise!" Diz exclaimed with a happy grin.

"Kalani!" The woman's voice had an urgent tone.

"I'm coming, Mom." The girl turned to the boys. "It's the short one. 'Bye, now!"

Josh wanted to cry, *No! Don't do it,* but Diz reached over the lanai and lifted the long board as the girl dashed inside. "Thanks!" Diz called to her.

Josh frowned. "I thought she said the short board."

"No, the long," Diz assured him, hoisting the board under his arm. "Come on! We're going to have fun!"

A little while later, Josh sat morosely on the white sand beach at Waikiki. "Whatever we do," Josh said to Tank who lay stretched out on the sand beside him, "we mustn't let anything happen to that board."

"It's sure a funny-looking one," Tank replied, turning to look toward the water where Diz lay sprawled along the length of the board. He was paddling with his hands toward deeper water with Roger and Manuel swimming on either side of him.

"It's made of some kind of wood, and it's extra long," Tank mused. "Maybe her father had it made special for her."

Josh was still uneasy, watching the other three boys giving Diz quick lessons in surfing. "Did you see the look on that girl's face when she mentioned her father? I have a hunch that her father is really strict."

Tank sat up. "Roger and Manuel are turning back, but Diz is still heading out to sea."

Josh got uneasily to his feet. "They shouldn't leave him alone like that. Come on! Let's go stop him."

The two best friends entered ankle-deep water just as Roger and Manuel splashed toward them in knee-high waves.

"Dat Mainland haole friend you got," Roger cried excitedly, waving his arms toward Diz, "he planty pupule!*"

"He says he's going to ride a wave in, but he's never even learned how to stand up on a surfboard," Manuel added. "Foolish, that's what he is."

Josh glanced in alarm toward where Diz was approaching the experienced surfers straddling their boards and waiting for the right set of waves. "Did you tell him about surfing rules?" Josh asked anxiously.

"Sure!" Roger replied. "We tried to tell him about which surfers have the right of way, and ... "

"Too late!" Josh interrupted. "Look! There's some big kid on a surfboard catching a wave and heading straight toward Diz. That's Kong!"

All four boys started jumping up and down, shouting and waving, but Diz kept going.

They fell silent, watching in fearful fascination as the inevitable happened. Kong, on his board, suddenly seemed to realize that Diz on his long board wasn't going to get out of the way. Kong cut back sharply to avoid hitting him, but lost his balance.

"Noooo!" Josh shrieked as Kong landed on the long board, bounced off, and disappeared under the water.

The collision also knocked Diz into the water, but he was a good swimmer in spite of his awkwardness on land. He surfaced, swam to his board, and started crawling back upon it. At the same time, Kong erupted from the sea, spitting saltwater and waving his huge arms like a madman. Diz didn't seem to notice, but started paddling toward shore, propelled by the incoming waves.

For a brief moment, Josh thought that Kong was going to be good-natured and continue surfing. But Kong let out an angry yell that could be heard on shore. Then Kong climbed on his board, took his stance, and caught the next wave. It propelled him directly toward Diz.

Tank moaned, turned away from the ocean, and covered his face with his hands. "When Kong catches Diz, he'll knock him into the middle of next week!"

"Maybe not!" Josh started running into deeper water. "Come on! Maybe if all of us explain to Kong, he'll ... "

"You're on your own!" Roger called.

Josh gulped but kept running as the water reached his knees. "While I talk to him, the rest of you grab the girl's surfboard! Don't let anything happen to it!"

The moment he said it, Josh wished he hadn't, because he suddenly had the strangest feeling that he was heading for more trouble than he imagined possible.

Chapter Four

A TERRIBLE MISTAKE

The water was up to Josh's knees when he met Diz wading toward shore with the long surfboard under his left arm.

"Wow, Josh!" Diz exclaimed with a broad smile. "Did you see me? I rode a surfboard on Waikiki Beach! Wait until I tell the kids back home!"

Josh glanced beyond Diz to where Kong was closing in fast from the sea, shoving his board ahead of him. He looked very angry.

"You got in Kong's way out there," Josh said, jerking his chin in the bully's direction.

Diz stopped in knee-deep water, holding the borrowed board so it wouldn't float away. "He tried to run over me with his surfboard."

"Didn't Roger and Manuel explain to you about which surfer has the right of way?"

"Sure, but that doesn't count when you get there first, does it?"

"It does when you're disputing the right of way with King Kong!" Josh watched the big boy reach shallow water and shove his board so it was carried on to the beach about thirty feet away. Josh asked hopefully, "Did you apologize to him?"

"What for?" Diz's voice held real surprise.

"It might have saved you from getting your face punched."

"He called me names."

"Like what?"

"I don't know, exactly. They sounded Hawaiian, but I'm sure they weren't nice words."

Josh wanted to run and urge Diz to do the same, but that would only have delayed the thumping. Kong wasn't considered very smart—very akamai—but his memory was long.

Josh watched apprehensively as Kong began wading through the shallow water, making great splashes.

Josh said to Diz, "I hope you didn't say anything back to him!"

"Not really." Diz didn't seem to be aware that the bully was coming up fast from behind. "I just said he was so big that he couldn't catch a fly if it was on the end of his nose. I also said . . . "

Josh yelled, "Stop! Don't say any more!" But it was too late. Kong was close enough to overhear. With a loud roar, and with nostrils flaring angrily, he reached both huge hands toward the back of Diz's scrawny neck.

For a second, Josh stood paralyzed, seeing Kong up close.

His left forearm was cut just inside the elbow. His massive right shoulder had been scraped over a six-inch-square area. His forehead bled from where he had hit some hidden coral after the inglorious dive off his surfboard. Most of all, he looked very angry.

Diz spun around to face Kong just as his fingers curled and descended like a striking snake toward Diz's long, skinny neck.

He reacted quickly, dropping the borrowed surfboard onto the surface of the water. He grabbed with his left hand to keep it from being swept away while his right arm lifted to ward off a blow. If it had landed, it would have been like a freight train going through a spider web. But Kong stopped abruptly, looking past Diz.

Josh swiveled his head around to see Tank, Roger, and Manuel hurrying toward them, splashing water everywhere.

"Kong," Manuel called. "There are five of us. Think about that!"

The bully hesitated, anger slowly fading from his eyes, but there was still a hot, fiery core there. When the three other boys joined Josh and Diz, Josh could almost hear the gears grinding slowly in Kong's head as he considered the situation.

After a tense moment, Kong smiled, shrugged those huge shoulders, and lowered both arms with their heavily muscled biceps. "Kong deal dis Mainland haole bumby.*" He snatched up Kalani's surfboard. "Kong keep dis, yeah?"

"Hey!" Josh yelled as Kong headed back toward his own surfboard. "That's not ours! We borrowed it! Please give it back."

"Too bad foh you guys," Kong called over his shoulder, picking up his own board. He strode off down the beach with a board tucked under each immense arm.

"That's stealing!" Diz shouted, but Kong didn't seem to hear. He kept on walking away with both boards.

Josh slowly turned to the other boys. "What'll we tell Kalani Gilhooley?"

"Yeah," Tank added, "and what will she tell her father?"

The thought made Josh's stomach turn, but he didn't have an answer.

Diz said with a hangdog expression, "It's my fault. I'll get her board back."

"You are pupule!" Roger cried. "Nobody can get anything from Kong except a faceful of his fists!"

"I've got to risk it," Diz insisted. He started after Kong.

"Wait!" Josh called. "You don't stand a chance against him. Even all of us couldn't take it away without somebody getting hurt. So we'd better go tell Kalani."

At the Gilhooley apartment, Josh rang the doorbell, hating what he had to report. Kalani opened the sliding screen door wearing a blue bathing suit.

"Oh," she said before Josh could say anything, "I'm glad you guys came back. There's been a terrible mistake. You took the wrong board."

"Wrong board?" Josh repeated.

"Yes," Kalani replied seriously. "I told you to take the short one, but you took the long one."

Diz protested, "I thought you said to take the long . . . "

"No! No!" Kalani shook her head vigorously, then asked anxiously, "Where is it?"

The boys exchanged glances before answering.

Josh explained briefly, hurting inside as the girl's brown eyes opened wide and her mouth dropped open.

"Oh!" she exclaimed in a small voice, her delicate hands flying to cover her mouth. "Can you get it back?"

Josh shook his head. "Not from Kong. But we'll buy you another . . . "

"No!" She dropped her hands. "You do not understand! That one once belong to Duke Kahanamoku.*"

Tank gasped. "*The* great Duke Kahanamoku? The father of modern surfing?"

Kalani nodded. "He gave it to my grandfather, who left it for my dad. He would never let anyone touch it. I would never have dared loan it. He will be furious when he gets home and it's not here."

Manuel asked, "How long before he gets back?"

"Just six days."

Diz said cheerfully, "I have to go back home in five days, so we can get it back before then, can't we, guys?"

"Not from Kong," Roger warned.

"Well," Diz told the girl, "don't you worry. It was my fault. I'll return it before your father gets home."

"Oh, thank you!" Hope sounded in Kalani's voice. Her eyes brightened and she smiled at him. "What's your name again—Daniel?"

"Yes, but most kids call me Diz."

"I like Daniel better, so I'll call you that," she said. "Daniel is one of my favorite people in the Bible. Daniel in the lions' den. You know the story?"

Diz nodded. "Heard it in Sunday school many times."

Tank said in his slow, easy way, "Now you're going to get a chance to live it out in real life, Diz. But I have got a hunch that the lions Daniel faced were kittens compared to what Kong will do if you try to get that board back from him."

"I have faith in you, Daniel," Kalani said softly, her voice warm and low. "But you'd better hurry. Six days will go fast."

After she closed the door, the boys walked away to discuss possible surfboard-recovery strategies. But nobody liked anybody else's ideas. Tensions rose, with sharp words directed at Diz for getting them into this mess.

Diz protested, "I don't understand why you're mad. Getting that surfboard back is the right thing to do, and because I lost it, I said I'd get it back. You guys don't even have to help."

"I'm worried about what Kong will do to you," Josh admitted, "but

I'm more concerned about what Kalani's father will do to her. Did you see the look in her eyes?"

"Yeah," Tank replied. "I'll bet he's mean to her."

"We can't let anything happen to her," Diz said slowly. He hesitated, then asked, "Do you guys think she's kind of cute?"

The other four boys looked at him as though he'd said something unspeakable.

"Cute?" Tank finally asked with a knowing wink at the other boys. "Diz thinks she's cute."

Tank laughed with Roger and Manuel, but Josh didn't. Still, he had to admit there was something different about Kalani.

Diz ignored the teasing. "You know what, guys? Maybe we could take the direct approach. All we have to do is explain to Kong about Kalani, and he'll give the board to us. No fuss."

All the other boys let out a collective groan.

"Sure," Roger said sarcastically, "we do that, and Kong will wrap that board around all our necks and set us out where the Polynesian Express* will carry us to Tahiti, if the sharks don't get us first."

"Let's all go to our rooms and try to think of good, workable ideas," Josh suggested. "Meantime, everybody stay away from Kong. That means you, too, Diz."

Spending time in his room with Disaster Davis turned out to be a trial for Josh. First Josh remembered the warning Victor had phoned him about some haole man on Molokai asking about him and Tank.

Whoever he is, Josh reminded himself, looking out the window every time he heard a car drive up the cul-de-sac, *he knows where we live. But who is he, and why does he want us?*

Josh was next distracted because Diz kept humming, whistling, drumming his fingers, and doing other annoying things. Each time

Josh asked Diz to stop, he apologized, saying it helped him to think. Moments later, he started cracking his knuckles.

Josh gritted his teeth, excused himself, and went into the living room.

His father looked up from where he sat in his favorite chair with the daily newspaper. He peered over the top of the silver-framed half-glasses he used when reading. "Something the matter, son?" he asked. "You look worried."

"Just thinking," Josh hedged, crossing toward the kitchen to get a cold drink.

Josh popped the top on his soda can, then started back into the living room. For a moment he thought about asking his father for suggestions on how to recover the borrowed surfboard. Josh's dad always listened, but he might also feel it was his fatherly duty to give a free lecture on responsibility with other people's property. Josh decided to not say anything—at least, not yet.

Still deep in his own thoughts, Josh took a sip of his soda as he headed back for his bedroom.

His father stopped him. "Wait, son. I have to go back to Molokai on business." He dropped the paper onto his lap and took off his glasses before continuing. "It'll be fast, in and out the same day. You want to come along?"

Did he? Josh would have jumped at the opportunity except for the time situation with Diz and the surfboard.

Mr. Ladd seemed to take his son's hesitancy as uncertainty. "I've got some advertising trade with an airline, so we can ride free," Mr. Ladd continued. "You can even take Tank and Diz along if you want."

Josh was anxious to return to the hidden heiau where he and Tank had been frightened off by the mysterious man with the scary voice. Maybe another visit would help uncover the truth behind the lights that Victor said were carried by the night walkers. But Josh was reluctant to lose a day of trying to recover the surfboard from Kong.

"Well?" Mr. Ladd prompted.

"Well, Dad . . . ," Josh stalled, but didn't get to say more.

Diz rushed down the hallway. "Did I hear you say we could go to one of the other islands, Mr. Ladd? I've never been to one. What'll we see? What'll we do?"

Josh realized he was stuck with taking Diz to Molokai, and he didn't want to do that. Instantly, Josh's conscience zapped him like a hot iron. *We have only four more days before Diz goes home. What if this lost day means we won't be able to get Kalani's surfboard back in time?*

While Mr. Ladd gave Diz a brief description of what the boys would see on Molokai, Josh ran downstairs to tell Tank. He lived in the apartment directly below the Ladds.

Tank sprawled barefooted before the television set. When Josh explained about the trip to Molokai, Tank leaped up. "Take Disaster Davis along? No way!"

"I've got no choice," Josh protested.

"Count me out."

Josh paused, thinking of something that always worked with his friend. "You afraid, Tank?"

"Me?" Tank spun around the room in mock anguish. "What's to be afraid of? Riding in an airplane with Diz? Going to a heiau where somebody with a sling gun doesn't want us? Maybe running into those night walkers with their spears? Of course I'm not afraid."

"Good!" Josh grinned good-naturedly at his friend. "I'm glad you're going along."

The next morning Mr. Ladd in his lightweight business suit drove the old family station wagon to the airport. Diz chattered excitedly away about his first flight on a smaller plane, but Josh and Tank were glumly silent and not a little fearful that they had a kind of Jonah riding with them.

They remained that way until the light aircraft landed at Molokai Airport at Hoolehua.* Mr. Ladd rented a car and headed toward the south shore.

"I wish we had more time, boys," he said. "We're not far from the famous leper* colony at Kalaupapa.* I've never had an opportunity to visit there, but I'd like to do that."

"Leper?" Diz asked. "Is that someone with the terrible disease in the Bible?"

"The same," Mr. Ladd agreed. "It's now called Hansen's Disease, and science knows how to control it. You boys know about Father Damien?"

Josh nodded. "He was the priest who went to Kalaupapa back when the disease was uncontrolled. While serving the lepers, Father Damien caught the disease and died there."

"He must have been some man," Diz said admiringly. "I'll have to read up on him when I get back home."

Moments after Mr. Ladd dropped the boys off at Victor's, he drove away. Victor wasted no time.

"Come on," he urged. "Let's go to the heiau. It should be safe in the daytime."

As the other three boys started to follow Victor, Josh heard Tank mumble under his breath, "Not with Disaster Davis along!"

Chapter Five

STRANGE CRIES IN THE NIGHT

The four boys hurried along the deserted rural road barely a hundred yards from the ocean.

Victor said, "Let's start at the place where we saw the night walkers' lights."

Josh and Tank agreed, then briefly filled Diz in on the details.

Victor said, "I hope you don't think that the reason I didn't go with you up the mountain that night was because I was scared."

Tank laughed. "No, we didn't *think* that. We *knew* it."

Diz said wistfully, "I wish I had been here that night."

Josh didn't say anything, but he was glad that Disaster Davis had not been there. In fact, Josh was a little nervous about Diz being here now.

Victor admitted, "Well, maybe I was scared, just a little bit. But then it was dark. Today it's clear and beautiful, and there's nothing to be scared of."

"No," Josh replied, "except the unknown."

"Yeah," Tank added, in his slow, thoughtful way. "But that's the most scary thing of all, and that's what we're dealing with here."

"Not necessarily," Josh answered. "I still think there's no such thing as night walkers."

Victor exclaimed, "But we saw their lights!"

"And what about that voice we heard?" Tank countered. "That didn't sound human to me."

"It sounded to me like somebody trying to scare us off that mountain," Josh replied, "which is what happened after we heard that sling gun go off in our direction."

Josh turned to Victor. "Tell me about this haole stranger who was asking your friends about Tank and me and where we live."

"Not much to tell. My friends said that he was medium sized and kind of ordinary looking."

Tank muttered, "That fits the description of half the world's population."

"They only saw him once," Victor added.

The boys lapsed into silence while the sun glistened off the water to their left. Even the mountain to the right, where the mysterious lights had been the other night, was bathed in warm sunlight. Hawaii's famous warm trade winds stirred the branches of thorny kiawe trees on the hill and rattled the palm fronds on the beach. It was a perfect day for exploring.

They took their bearings at the campfire site and decided about where they had seen the lights coming down the mountainside. Then, with Josh leading, they headed up the hill where Josh and Tank had gone before they heard the warning voice.

All four boys were perspiring and panting before they had climbed more than about fifteen minutes up the mountain's sloping side. They stopped to catch their breath and to look for anything familiar. But nothing looked the same as it had at night.

"We'll just keep going," Josh decided. "It's got to be around here somewhere."

"What has?" Diz asked, tripping over a trailing vine and almost falling headlong into the underbrush. "That scary voice, that old heiau, or the characters with the flaming torches?"

"Take your pick," Josh replied. "We stumbled into . . . " He broke off abruptly, stopped, and held up his hands for silence.

For a moment, the only sound was their hard breathing. Then Josh pointed. "Over there. Through the trees and vines. I think I see part of the heiau."

Carefully, the boys eased forward, frequently stopping to listen and to find ways through the increasing tangle of lilikoi vines* and thorny kiawe trees. They reached the heiau's base and looked up at the black volcanic rock.

"Well, at least we found this," Josh said, seeking to find hand- and footholds in the wall-like base. "Let's see what we can spot up on top."

Puffing hard, the boys scrambled onto the vast expanse of rock and looked around. Josh marveled that ancient Hawaiians had the patience to build a platform about a hundred feet square. But he could see why it had been chosen as a place of worship.

To the south, the ocean spread out like melted silver, reaching from the shoreline toward the horizon. In other directions, silent jungle-like growth stretched out with occasional bursts of many-colored flowers. It was beautiful, serene, and totally isolated.

"I've seen lots of heiaus in these islands," Josh said quietly, "but none as hidden as this one."

"Sort of reminds me of an asphalt parking lot," Diz commented, "except this one's made of these funny black rocks." He bent and picked up a couple to examine more closely.

"They're volcanic," Josh explained. "Careful, or you'll cut yourself. They're pretty rough."

"Think I'll just take these home to show my friends in California," Diz announced. He started to stuff them into the front pockets of his cutoffs.

"No!" Victor cried, reaching out to stop him. "You can't do that!"

"Sure I can," Diz said. "These are just the right size to fit . . . "

Josh interrupted, "Victor's trying to tell you that you're not supposed to take rocks from heiaus."

"Oh, I get it," Diz said. He stopped trying to put the rocks in his pockets and examined them again. "Environmental stuff."

"If you take the rocks," Victor explained, "the menehunes will come at night and cry outside your room until you give them back."

"Menehunes?" Diz scratched his head with one rock. "Aren't they those little people like leprechauns* or elves that the Hawaiians believed in?"

"Some still do," Josh assured him.

"Well, I don't, so I think I will take these home with me," Diz replied. He again started shoving the rocks into his pockets.

Josh suggested, "Out of respect for Victor's beliefs, why don't you leave the rocks here?"

Diz replied, "Well, if you put it that way . . . " He broke off his sentence and froze, staring into the trees beyond the heiau.

"What'd you see?" Josh asked, trying to probe the trees where Diz was looking.

"There was somebody over there." Diz's voice had dropped to a whisper.

"Where?" Josh asked, frantically looking around.

Diz said, "By that big tree, but he's gone now."

"Come on," Josh said, sprinting across the rough heiau stones. "Let's try to find out who it is."

"I think he was watching us," Diz said, running behind Josh, Tank, and Victor. "I wonder why?"

Josh didn't know, but he surely wanted to find out. He reached the end of the heiau, scrambled down the wall, and plunged through the brush with the other boys close behind.

They had gone only fifty feet when they burst into a small clearing. Josh stopped, panting, in the middle of a narrow, almost invisible trail.

"This must be where we saw those strange lights the other night," he explained, glancing quickly up and down the trail to where it vanished into the trees in both directions. "Let's see where this leads."

"Up or down?" Diz asked. "It goes both ways, and we can't go both directions at once, you know."

"Down," Victor said firmly. "Let's find out where it leads."

Josh, Tank, and Diz agreed. After they knew where it originated, they could later start there and follow the trail up the mountain to see where it ended.

The boys kept a wary eye out for whoever had been watching them. They didn't see anybody, but soon came upon a few footprints, which the boys stopped to examine.

"Not locals," Victor announced.

Diz challenged, "How do you know that?"

"No bare feet," Victor pointed out. "Whoever made these wore regular shoes, not tennis shoes or slippahs.*" He used the local pronunciation of slippers, or sandals. He added, "Haoles, most likely."

Josh knelt to check the prints carefully. "These weren't made recently, so whoever Diz saw didn't go this way. Those blades of grass are standing upright, but if they'd just been stepped on, they'd still be bent over, or still straightening up."

"So where did the guy that I saw go?" Diz asked.

"Let's try to find out," Josh answered, and started down the narrow trail again. The other boys followed single file.

As they neared the end of the mountain's slope, Josh slowed and moved cautiously. He caught glimpses of the rural road through the trees, but there wasn't a single vehicle in sight. *Sure is quiet and lonely,* he thought with some concern.

About a hundred yards off the road, Josh expected to see the path break out of the trees onto the roadway. But it didn't. The trail led straight toward what seemed to be a solid wall of trees and brush. As Josh carefully pushed them aside, he stopped in surprise.

"It's the opening to a cave," Tank whispered.

Josh shook his head. "No, I think it's one of those lava tubes.*"

They were common in Hawaii, he knew. They had been made centuries ago when molten lava cooled faster on the surface, forming a kind of tube through which the hotter interior magma continued to flow. Over time, the interior had drained, leaving another hollow tube. Some of them were big enough to crawl through.

Josh turned to the other three boys. "It is very dark inside, and we don't have a light, so I can't see much. I can't see daylight on the other side, so either it's very long and deep, or there's a door or something blocking it that I can't make out from here. But I'd like to see where it goes."

"To the ocean, I'll bet," Tank guessed. "It's not more than a few hundred feet from here."

"Can't go to the ocean," Victor disagreed. "My friends and I have walked every inch of that shoreline a thousand times."

"There's one way to find out," Josh mused. "Victor, have you got a flashlight at home?"

"Sure. We could go get . . . "

Whoosh!

Victor broke off his sentence as something whizzed over the boys' heads. A second later, a spear from a sling gun quivered in a tree trunk ahead of them.

All four boys whirled around, but there was nobody in sight. There was not a sound or movement of brush or trees to show where their attacker was hidden.

"Let's get out of here!" Josh cried, leaping up. He left the trail and plunged into the trees, circling the hidden cave entrance, then headed straight for the road. The other boys crashed noisily behind him.

They reached the pavement and stopped in the middle of it, breathing hard from fright and exertion. Then they silently turned to peer into the bushy hillside where they had been moments before.

"Nothing," Tank said in a low tone. "There's not a sign of the trail or the cave or anything."

Josh glanced around, looking for landmarks so he could find the place again. "Well, now we know where the trail starts," he observed. "And we know about the cave or lava tube. But it's not safe to get lights and come back here today—not with somebody hiding up there holding a sling gun."

"But," Tank pointed out, "your dad's coming for us later today, so we can't be here tomorrow."

Victor said fervently, "Well, I'm not going near there by myself."

"We better talk about this some more," Diz said.

The others agreed, but by the time they had reached Victor's home, they had not reached a decision. They sat under a huge monkeypod tree* to decide what to do next.

"Ouch," Diz exclaimed as he eased down. "These rocks are really rough."

Josh and the other boys turned in surprise as Diz fished the volcanic rocks from his pockets.

"Hey!" Victor cried. "I thought you left those behind!"

"I started to," Diz admitted, "but forgot all about them when I saw that guy move, and we started running."

Victor sadly shook his head. "Now you've done it!"

"Aw," Diz scoffed. "Don't worry, Victor. Your little menehunes won't miss these two little old rocks."

Josh suggested, "Don't tease, Diz. You should have respected Victor's wishes."

"I intended to, Josh, but you know what happened."

"Doesn't matter about that," Victor said in a voice filled with concern. "I just hope the menehunes don't come for those rocks tonight."

"No problem," Diz replied. "Josh, Tank, and I won't be here, and those little creatures won't know where to find these rocks in Honolulu."

Just then the phone rang. Mrs. Aka answered it, listened, and said, "Of course. No problem." Then she handed the instrument to Josh. "It's your father."

"Son, something important has come up, so I've got to stay over until tomorrow," he explained. "Mrs. Aka says you boys are welcome to spend the night, and I'll pick all of you up tomorrow afternoon. I'll call your mother and let her know."

Josh had mixed feelings when he hung up the phone. He was glad to have an opportunity to take a flashlight tomorrow and try to look into the cave or tube. But it also meant another of the precious four remaining days would be lost for recovering Kalani's surfboard from Kong.

He told Diz, "You can return those rocks tomorrow."

Victor warned, "The menehunes may not like them to be gone for even one night."

Victor's family didn't own much, but they had the true old aloha spirit.* At bedtime, Mrs. Aka spread beach mats on the floor of her son's room.

Victor offered to give up his bottom bunk to one of the boys, but they wouldn't let him. Tank took the top bunk. Josh and Diz each spread old beach towels on the mats to sleep on the floor. It wasn't bad, Josh found, as he stretched out. He was young and his body was tired, so he knew he could sleep.

For a while Josh and the other boys discussed ways of recovering the surfboard that Kong had taken.

Diz suggested, "We could try distracting Kong. Like if we know where he keeps the surfboard, you guys could get his attention while I run up and grab it."

"That's a brave thing to try, Diz, but it wouldn't work," Josh said. "He'd come get it back and then catch us alone, one by one, and beat up on us. We've got to find a way to make him *want* to give it back—and soon."

The other boys agreed, but nobody had any ideas on how to do that, and the clock was racing against them. Josh absently watched a gecko lizard on the screen snatching up bugs that tried to get into the light, but his thoughts were elsewhere. He reviewed the strange events of the day and was grateful that nobody had been hurt. He was especially glad that Diz hadn't done anything disastrous. Except for carrying away the heiau rocks, he had not even done anything wrong.

Finally, everyone said goodnight, and the lights were turned out. Josh was lulled to sleep by the distant sound of the surf.

He was awakened by someone shaking his shoulder. He opened his eyes in total darkness. Someone was crouching over him.

"It's me, Diz," the boy whispered. "Wake up, Josh."

He awakened instantly, all sleep gone. "What's the matter?" he whispered back.

"Listen!"

Josh propped himself up on one knee, listening hard and trying to make out the other boys in the room. It was so dark that he could see only dark shapeless forms.

"Hear it?" Diz whispered.

At first, Josh heard only Diz's frightened and ragged breathing in the totally darkened room. Then Josh heard something else through the screen window, and the short hairs on the back of his neck stood up.

Chapter Six

A SECRET UNCOVERED

Through the window came an unearthly wailing. It sounded a little like cats fighting on a fence, only more scary. There was also a hint of howling, like wolves in the distance. Yet the sounds were all mixed up, unlike anything Josh had ever heard.

"Hear them?" Diz whispered. "It's them, I tell you! The menehunes! Josh, I'm sorry I took their rocks!" Diz's voice quavered. "What'll I do?"

Josh didn't answer. He reminded himself that there were no such things as menehunes. He glanced toward the stacked bunk beds where Tank and Victor slept.

It was too dark to make out even the outline of the beds, but Josh heard Tank roll over heavily in the top bunk and begin snoring loudly. For a moment, Josh thought of awakening him and Victor, but decided against that.

Taking a deep breath, Josh eased off his sleeping mat and started crawling across the floor toward the window.

"Don't go!" Diz whispered, his voice a frightened croak. "Stay away from there!"

"If they existed, which I don't believe," Josh whispered back, "menehunes wouldn't hurt anybody." His logical mind helped to ease the initial sense of fear. He added, "They're just supposed to be mischievous."

At the open window, Josh cupped his hands on both sides of his eyes and eased against the screen. He hoped the little gecko was no longer there, although it was harmless. Josh strained to see outside.

There was no moon, and the massive bulk of the monkeypod tree made the night seem even darker. The weird cries broke off suddenly. Except for the muted sound of the distant surf, total silence settled over the area.

"Whew!" Diz whispered with relief, his voice inches away from Josh's ear. "I never want to hear anything like that again. Do you think they'll come back?"

Josh glanced across the room where the sound of Tank's heavy snoring continued. "I doubt it," Josh whispered back. "Now, let's get some sleep."

"I'll try, but tomorrow, first thing, I'm going to return these rocks, and I'm never ever going to do anything like that again."

Josh smiled in the darkness and crawled back to his sleeping mat, where he passed the rest of the night in silence.

The next morning, Diz surprised Josh by not even mentioning the night sounds to Tank or Victor. Josh waited until Victor was alone and then sidled up to him. "Your little scheme worked," Josh said with a smile.

Victor grinned broadly. "How'd you know I did it?"

"It took me a little while to figure it out, but when I heard Tank snoring so hard I couldn't even hear if you were breathing, it came to me."

"Was I pretty good?"

Josh laughed and playfully punched the other boy on his shoulder.

"You were terrific! I never heard anything more terrifying."

"Not even that scary voice you and Tank heard the other night on that mountain?"

"Yours was much worse," Josh assured Victor. "But now that I know what made those sounds outside your house last night, I've got to know about those on the mountain. How soon can we go there?"

After breakfast, and armed with two small flashlights, the four boys headed back to where they had seen the entrance to the cave or lava tube. On the way, Diz was strangely quiet.

Finally he said, "I want you guys to know I'm bringing these black stones with me. So let's not forget to go to the heiau so I can put them back where I found them."

Victor said with a straight face, "Something happen to make you want to do that, Diz?"

"Let's just say I decided it's best, that's all."

Josh and Victor exchanged knowing glances, and both had to stifle laughter. Tank, who wasn't in on the situation, looked at them strangely.

Josh silently mouthed the words, "*Tell you later.*" Tank nodded, seeming to understand.

As they walked on along the deserted rural road, Josh said, "Kalani's father returns in just a few days. Any of you think of a way to get that surfboard back from Kong?"

"I've thought so hard my brain is sore," Tank replied.

Diz asked seriously, "How can a brain be sore?"

"It was just an expression," Tank explained.

"Oh." Diz looked thoughtful. "I've been thinking about that surfboard, too, but I don't think my brain is sore. Maybe I need to think harder."

"By the time we get home," Josh reminded them, "we'll have almost no time left. I hate to think what Kalani's father is going to say to her, and to us."

"Us?" Tank exclaimed. "We didn't lose that board! Kong took it. Well, he really stole it."

"But we're responsible," Josh said quietly.

"Actually," Diz said, "I'm the one who's responsible. If Mr. Gilhooley is going to be mad and yell at anybody, it should be me."

"You'll be safely back on the Mainland," Tank pointed out. "Josh and I will get the blame."

"Can't let that happen." Diz spoke solemnly. "You both have been so good to me, even back in California. All the other kids picked on me, but you two were about my only friends in . . . " Diz's voice broke.

Josh and Tank exchanged glances. They both knew Diz's background. His parents were professional people who had once told their son that they had not planned on having a child because they needed to be gone a lot on business. They had not expected Diz, and when he was old enough, they sent him to a military academy, claiming it was best for him. But Diz had confided to Josh and Tank that he thought his parents really didn't want him around.

Then Josh lightly slapped Diz on the shoulder. "We'll find a way to get that board back before the deadline."

"You think so?" Diz's face lit up.

Josh nodded, hearing Tank groan under his breath. "Let's keep thinking. Meanwhile, we'd better try to figure out about these lights and the other mysterious things that have been going on here."

The three other boys agreed. Josh said thoughtfully, "I enjoy studying local beliefs. Maybe that comes from having a father who used to teach high school history, and is always having us look things up.

"I heard about menehunes even before we moved to Hawaii, but I never heard about night walkers. When I get back to the apartment, I'm going to look them up in my Hawaiian dictionary."

Tank commented, "Good idea. I wouldn't be surprised if they're not even listed."

Victor protested, "But you both saw the lights coming down the mountain the other night. You heard that voice saying that was a kapu area. How can you not believe?"

"Belief is a very powerful thing," Josh replied. "We can even fool ourselves sometimes. I'm convinced that there's something fishy about this whole thing, and having those two spear guns fired in our direction makes me even more sure."

"Well, I guess we'll soon find out," Tank said. "Right up ahead is where it happened yesterday."

Not a single car had met or passed the boys on the narrow roadway, which added to the sense of remoteness and loneliness of the area. The boys fell silent as they left asphalt pavement and slipped up through the trees and brush to where the trail down the mountain ended.

The undergrowth hid the cave's entrance, just as it had yesterday. There was nothing to indicate what was behind the shrubbery. Nobody or nothing moved, so there was a strange, almost eerie, stillness.

"Well," Josh said in a low voice, "let's take those flashlights and see what's down there."

"Wait!" Tank whispered. Always the cautious one, he added hastily, "What about the spear that was shot at us yesterday? Maybe whoever did it is still around."

"Maybe," Josh agreed, "but I'm going to look. The rest of you can wait here if you want." He reached over and took one of the flashlights from Victor. "Be right back," he said.

He had taken only a few steps when the others whispered for him to wait. They followed him down the incline to where the faint mountain trail ended at the entrance to the cave or lava tube.

Josh felt himself tense with anticipation as he slowly reached out with his left hand and pulled the shrubbery aside. The same dark and forbidding entrance was again revealed. With his right hand, Josh thrust the flashlight forward and snapped it on.

Behind him, one of the boys sucked in his breath so sharply Josh whispered, "Shh!"

The opening was obviously an ancient lava tube about four feet high. The rough edges testified to that. But the solid black metal gate with the heavy padlock located three feet inside the tube was definitely man-made.

Josh played the light over the gate and stepped closer to examine the lock. Then he turned, snapped off the light, and motioned for the other boys to retreat.

Outside on the faint trail again, Tank grumbled, "There's no way we can get beyond that gate. Now what will we do?"

Josh suggested, "Let's follow the trail back up the mountain and see where it goes."

"What if somebody's up there waiting?" Tank asked.

"Good question," Diz said. "Remember, I saw someone watching us yesterday, and then there was that spear . . . "

"We'll be careful," Josh interrupted. "You see, I don't think those spears were meant to hit us."

"You don't?" Tank asked.

"No, I don't. We were close enough both times that if the shooter wanted to hit us, he could have. I think somebody's just trying to scare us off." He started up the trail.

"Well," Tank admitted, "I'm not afraid to say I'm scared."

"Then why are you coming?" Victor asked. "You and I could go back to the road and wait."

Josh stopped in the path, studying his friends. He knew that Tank would follow in spite of his fears. But Victor came from a different background of beliefs that made him fear things that didn't frighten Josh. He didn't want to embarrass Victor.

Josh said, "I think that's a good idea. You can be our lookout on the roadway and shout if you see any danger for Tank and me." Josh saw the relief on Victor's face, so he added, "Diz, why don't you go with him?"

Tank whispered under his breath, "Good thinking, Josh! We'll be safer without him tagging along."

Diz had other ideas. "Thanks, fellows, but I can't. I have got to return these ol' rocks to that heiau."

"I'll take them for you," Josh volunteered.

"Yeah," Tank added quickly, "we'll return them."

"That's nice of you two," Diz replied, "but it wouldn't be right. I took them, so I'll return them."

"It's not necessary," Tank protested. "We'll ... "

"Sorry, guys, but I made up my mind," Diz said solemnly. "So let's get going."

Josh glanced at Victor, who took a slow breath, then let it out before nodding. "He's right. Let's all go."

They found the heiau without difficulty and climbed up on it. Josh stood silently, gazing in all directions. Through the tangle of vines and trees that hid the ancient temple site from outside view, Josh could see the ocean below and hear the trade winds rustling nearby tree leaves.

"Sure is a pretty spot," Diz commented.

"Sure is," Victor replied, glancing nervously around. "But you'd better drop those rocks so we can get out of here. Whoever was watching us yesterday might still be around, and this time he might be mad at us."

"Good idea," Diz agreed. "I'll just put them right back in the spot where I found them, near as I can tell."

"That's not necessary," Victor protested. "Just drop them and . . ."

"No, no!" Diz interrupted. "I want to do this right so there won't be any more . . ." He caught himself, broke off his thought, and glanced anxiously at Tank and Victor.

"Any more what?" Tank prompted.

Josh, realizing that Diz didn't want to risk hearing any more strange cries in the night, spoke up. "Never mind, Tank. Diz, you go ahead."

He took out the stones and started walking toward the place where he had picked them up.

"What's going on?" Tank asked as Josh and Victor exchanged knowing glances.

"You want to tell him, Victor?"

"Why not?" he replied, and quickly told about having sneaked out of the house last night and scared Diz with the sounds he attributed to menehunes.

Tank started to laugh just as Diz let out a frightened yell. "Ohhhhhh!"

The other three boys whirled around just in time to see Diz trip at the high end of the heiau. He stood on the cliff-like edge, long arms threshing violently in an effort to regain his balance.

"Look out!" Josh cried, starting to run toward Diz.

"Don't fall over . . . ," Tank shouted, but didn't finish his thought.

Diz toppled like a broken windmill over the heiau's side and disappeared from sight.

Chapter SEVEN

FINAL WARNING

Josh led the other boys in a frantic dash across the rough black lava heiau. Fearful of what he would find, Josh slowed, panting hard, and peered over the high end of the ancient temple grounds.

Disaster Davis lay still on the ground twelve feet below.

"Oh, no!" Tank whispered, standing with Victor at Josh's side.

Josh shifted his eyes from the frightening scene below to the face of the heiau wall.

"Let's see if we can climb down," he said, sitting down and dangling his feet over the edge. Then he twisted around and got a good grip on the top of the heiau wall. He added, "Feel for footholds between the rocks. Don't slip."

He ignored the pain in his fingers as the rough volcanic stones cut into them. His knees scraped against the wall as he glanced down, trying to see places where he could place his feet. That was fairly easy because the rocks had been set without mortar countless years before.

When his feet were about five feet above the ground, he gave himself a little shove away from the wall, released his grip, and fell beside Diz's still form.

Tank and Victor did the same. All three boys knelt beside Diz, whose fall had been cushioned by the dense brush that grew against the sides of the heiau. Josh started to turn Diz's face up, fearful of seeing something terrible.

Instead, Diz looked up at him and smiled weakly.

"Are you all right?" Josh asked, anxiety mixed with relief making his voice rise.

Slowly, Diz pulled his long legs under himself and rolled to a sitting position. "Just got the wind knocked out of me, I guess."

"You've also got some cuts on your forehead, and your right arm is skinned," Josh replied.

"Yeah," Tank added, "you look like you got into a fight with a big old tomcat, and you lost."

Diz managed a grin. "It's nothing serious."

"It is to us," Tank exclaimed, "because you scared us to death!"

"I'm sorry about that," Diz apologized, reaching into his pockets. "Maybe I shouldn't have tried to keep these, after all." He held up the two heiau rocks he had picked up on his last trip.

Josh scowled. "I thought you were going to put them back."

"I was," Diz admitted, thoughtfully studying the stones, "but then I got to thinking that I don't believe in menehunes like you do, Victor."

"So you kept them again," Tank grumbled.

"I sure did," Diz confessed.

"And look what happened," Victor scolded. "You could have busted your head, or broken an arm or leg."

"Falling had nothing to do with these rocks," Diz began, but stopped when Josh suddenly grabbed his arms and held up his other hand.

"Listen!" Josh whispered, tensing and glancing around.

The other three boys fell silent.

The trade winds had brought a faint sound, but Josh couldn't tell what it was or where it was coming from. His blue eyes flickered over the mountainside at an angle he had never before experienced. He could see under some of the trees to the ocean.

Tank whispered, "I don't hear anything."

"Me either," Diz added, and Victor nodded in agreement.

"It's gone now," Josh said, "but it sounded like a motor, maybe a truck."

Victor scoffed, "There's no road up here on this mountainside."

"There are off-road vehicles that could travel up here," Josh pointed out.

The boys listened for about a minute more. Then Josh shrugged. "Well, I guess it wasn't important. Come on, let's get back to the road."

"Not before Diz throws those stones down," Victor declared solemnly.

Diz looked at the rough black rocks in his hands and sighed. "I sure would like to take them back to Los Angeles with me, but . . . "

"Shh!" Josh interrupted. "I *do* hear something."

"It's your imagination again," Tank teased.

"No!" Josh pointed down the heiau's wall. "There's a man near the far end!"

"He's wearing a wet suit!" Tank exclaimed. "But why? There's no water up here."

"Shh!" Josh repeated.

Although it was perhaps a mile up the side of the mountain away from the ocean, they could see a bald man in a black scuba-diver's suit. It covered him from ankles to neck as he walked toward the heiau. He effortlessly carried something resembling a large metal suitcase in his left hand. In his right, he held a sling gun.

Tank asked hoarsely, "Where did he come from?"

"Out of nowhere," Victor answered softly.

Tank replied, "I think maybe he was in that truck or whatever Josh thought he . . . "

"No, he came from the heiau," Josh replied.

"Then how come we didn't see him?" Tank wanted to know.

The bald man stopped suddenly and whirled around, glancing to where the boys crouched in the underbrush.

"He heard us!" Tank hissed.

"Be quiet!" Josh urged.

But it was too late. The man set the metal case down carefully and gripped the spear gun with both hands. Slowly, he started advancing toward the boys.

"Better stand up and explain," Josh said, stepping out into the open.

"Stop right there!" The man's voice froze all the boys in their tracks.

"It's okay, mister," Josh called. "My friends and I were just out exploring . . . "

"Not around here!" the stranger broke in, waving his left hand while the other held the weapon. "Get out of here!"

"Great idea!" Tank replied.

"Wait!" Josh said quietly. He raised his voice. "Look, mister, this is public property, isn't it? We have as much right . . . "

"Don't smart-mouth me, you pupule haole," the man yelled. "Get out of here and don't ever come back, or you'll be sorry! This is your only warning, and it's final! Do you hear me?"

"Yes, but . . . ," Josh objected, then stopped when the man started toward them, spear gun in hand. "Let's go," Josh said, turning and giving Tank and Diz a shove on their shoulders.

"I'm already gone," Tank assured him, turning away.

Josh didn't like running away, but his common sense told him that even soldiers sometimes temporarily retreated.

The boys did not have to run back across the heiau, but dashed around the corner. They avoided the heavy brush that grew solidly against the walls. When they came to the high back end where they had climbed up, they sprinted away from the heiau to the narrow path. They pounded down it, single file, with Victor leading. He was followed by Diz, Tank, and Josh.

Puffing hard, the boys reached the roadway somewhat scratched and cut from hastily taking shortcuts through thorny kiawe trees. There they paused in the middle of the deserted and lonely roadway to look back up the mountainside.

Diz asked thoughtfully, "Who do you suppose he was, and why did he run us off?"

"Yeah," Tank added, "and what was he doing in a wet suit that far from the ocean?"

"Good questions," Josh admitted. "We'd better think about them while we head back to Victor's house. My dad will be there to pick us up pretty soon."

When the boys reached Victor's home, Josh had thought through some points. "If that was a truck or off-road vehicle I heard back there, that could explain how the man got up there in a wet suit."

"But why would he wear one of those," Tank mused, "or have a truck or something up there on that mountain?"

"What I want to know," Diz said, "is why he ran us off when we weren't doing anything?"

"Because," Josh guessed, "he must have been doing something illegal and doesn't want us around."

"I'll tell my parents, and they'll call the police again," Victor said. "But the last time, the police didn't find anything, so maybe they won't even come out this time."

"You can tell about the cave or lava tube with the gate," Diz said, "and what happened today. That'll give the police something to go on."

"Yes, but unless they can find some illegal activity," Tank said, "I don't think the police can do a thing."

"Then we'll just have to do it ourselves," Josh replied firmly.

Tank groaned and bent over in mock pain. "I can't believe you'd go back up there, Josh!"

"Maybe he won't have to," Diz said. "Now, if you three don't mind, I'd like to get off this subject and try to think how to get Kalani's board back from Kong before her father returns home."

"Yes," Josh agreed. "We have got to do more than just think. Time's almost gone, so we've got to act fast."

On the flight back to Honolulu that afternoon, Josh told his father about the morning's experience.

"Son," Mr. Ladd said, "you may have a legal right to be there, but if that man is doing something illegal, you could be in danger. I don't want you going back up there."

"Oh, Dad! I'll be careful."

"I love you too much to let you risk your life unnecessarily, or those of your friends." Josh's father glanced at Tank and Diz sitting across the aisle from them.

Tank obviously overheard, because he turned with a satisfied grin to face Diz. "Did you hear . . . ?" He broke off when his eyes fell on something in Diz's hands.

"You still got those heiau rocks?" he asked in surprise.

"I was going to leave them, but that man started yelling at us, so I forgot them and took off running with the rest of you guys."

"Well, get rid of them!" Tank ordered.

"I can't just throw them away! I have to return them to where I found them. Victor said so!"

Tank sighed, then muttered, "We'll ask Josh, but not in front of his dad. Wait until we get home."

Diz slumped glumly in his seat. "When I get there, I have more important things to do."

"Yeah? What?"

"I have to start doing something to get Kalani's surfboard back from King Kong."

"You let him hear you call him that," Tank warned, "and you'll never be able to do anything else—ever."

As the old station wagon pulled into the carport, Manuel and Roger were watching another local boy husking a coconut on a spike driven through a board. Roger and Manuel hurried over to greet the new arrivals. Mr. Ladd cordially greeted them, then went into the apartment, leaving the boys alone.

Diz looked hopefully at Roger and Manuel. "Any luck getting that board back from Kong?"

"We're still healthy," Manuel replied. "What does that tell you?"

Diz seemed confused, so Josh explained. "They mean they haven't been near Kong."

Manuel nodded soberly. "And he hasn't been near us, for which I'm glad."

"How about Kalani?" Diz asked, glancing toward her ground-floor apartment in the adjacent building.

Roger playfully nudged Diz with an elbow and lapsed into pidgin English. "Dat wahine, she got eyes foh you, yeah? All time ask 'bout you."

Manuel flashed a teasing grin. "That's right. She doesn't ask about Josh, Tank, or Roger and me—just Daniel, as she calls him."

"She's anxious about getting her board back," Diz said. "I'd better go talk to her."

"Better hurry before her father comes back," Manuel warned. "I bet he's got a temper and eats malihinis* for breakfast—especially if that malihini let Kong take his favorite surfboard." Diz slowly walked away.

"Poor Diz," Tank said in his slow way. "I feel sorry for him."

"Moh bettah you be sorry foh yo'se'f, bruddah!" Roger exclaimed. "Dat Diz, he nothin' but long arms and legs, but dah wahine have much aloha* foh him! How come? We all bettah lookin' dan he!"

All except Josh agreed. Josh said soberly, "Maybe she sees something in him that we don't see."

"Then she sure has better eyesight than I have," Manuel declared with a shake of his head. "But enough about Diz. Tell us about your trip to Molokai."

Josh and Tank complied, but an excited retelling of the dramatic events on the other island couldn't compete with what Disaster Davis was doing. Josh, Tank, Roger, and Manuel watched as Diz knocked on Kalani's door and she opened it.

Josh and the other boys couldn't hear her greeting, but they saw her smile. It was big and warm, and Diz met her eyes only briefly, then looked down at his feet.

"Look at him," Tank grumbled. "Standing there digging his toes into the doormat like a bashful country boy with a pretty girl."

"Oh, Tank," Manuel said, "you're just wishing that was you instead of him getting that big smile."

"You're pupule, Manuel!" Tank replied sharply. "I just wish he'd go back to Los Angeles. He's caused us enough trouble."

Josh glanced at his best friend. "I've never heard you talk like that."

"Well, he's starting to rub me wrong," Tank defended himself. "He got us into this mess with Kong. Oh, and you know what else Diz has done?" Without waiting for a response, Tank explained, "He brought those rocks back from the heiau again."

When Josh started to protest, Tank hurriedly repeated the explanation Diz had given him on the plane.

Roger's eyes widened. "Ho! Too bad, yeah? Now we all got planty moh pilikia*—more trouble."

"Now, guys," Josh protested, "you're making too much of these stones. They don't have anything to do with the problems we're having . . . Let's drop it. Here comes Diz."

"Yeah," Tank said under his breath as Diz turned away from Kalani.

She waved and smiled at the other boys, but it wasn't the same as the one she had reserved for Diz. Tank continued, "Look at that silly grin on his face. He acts as if he were floating on air."

Roger lowered his voice and switched back to proper English. "Good thing, too. He's walking so fast he's about to get those long legs all tangled up."

"Oh, come on," Josh pleaded. "He's really a very nice guy, so let's not pick on him."

"Just the same," Roger replied sourly, "I'd like to take him on a snipe hunt, Hawaiian style. A little harmless trick might be good for him. What do you guys say? Should we do it?"

Before they could reply, Josh shushed them because Diz was close enough to hear. His face was flushed and his eyes bright with excitement.

"Guess what?" he called while still several feet away. "Kalani's really scared of her father, but she's being so nice about the surfboard that I told her I'd try to get it back from Kong tonight."

Tank made a strangled sound. "You what?"

"Told her I'd get it back from Kong . . . "

Tank interrupted angrily, "Tonight? That's impossible, Diz!"

"We've got to try," he answered lamely.

Tank groaned in dismay.

The other three boys echoed the groan.

Chapter Eight

A RASH PROMISE

Josh, Tank, Roger, and Manuel broke off their groaning and impaled Disaster Davis with hard looks.

Tank sputtered in utter disbelief, "I still can't believe you told her that!"

Diz protested, "Oh, come on, guys! You all said that you'd help me get the board back. So far, all we've done is talk about it. Now let's *do* something."

Josh struggled to keep his annoyance from showing in his face. He thought, *Diz had no right to tell Kalani that we'd get that surfboard back from King Kong tonight. We haven't even been able to think of a plan that might work.* Aloud, Josh asked, "What do you suggest, Diz?"

"Well," he replied thoughtfully, "one of us could call him on the phone and tell him the truth about that board. You know, appeal to his good side."

"Good side?" Roger hooted, slapping his thigh. "That's a good one! I've known Kong for years, and I've never heard anybody say that he has a good side."

Diz asked coolly, "Then what do you suggest?"

Josh watched Roger as he turned to Manuel and Tank to mouth something. Josh frowned, thinking Roger was silently forming the words, "snipe hunt," just as Mrs. Ladd called from the second-story lanai.

"Telephone, Josh. It's your father calling from the office. He says it's important."

As Josh ran toward the apartment building, Roger got a strange look in his eye. "Diz," he said in a friendly tone, "I just thought of something that might work."

Tank's eyes narrowed suspiciously, and Manuel lifted his eyebrows as though he had some doubts about what Roger was going to say.

"I'm listening," Diz replied.

"Well," Roger continued, turning his head so that Diz couldn't see him wink at Tank and Manuel, "first, I have to ask you a question. You ever eat frog legs?"

"Once," Diz admitted. "When I came home from military academy, and my father was in a good mood, he took me to a fancy restaurant. We ordered frog legs."

"Did you enjoy them?" Roger asked.

"As I remember, they were okay. Why?"

Roger seemed to be suppressing a grin. "Well, I happen to know that frog legs are Kong's favorite food."

"They are?"

"Oh, yes," Roger assured Diz in a solemn tone.

"Say!" Diz exclaimed. "Maybe we could go down to the market and buy some frog legs and give them to Kong."

"No need to do that," Roger said. "There are hundreds of frogs around here . . . "

"Toads," Manuel interrupted. "Those are . . . "

"Hawaiian frogs," Roger finished quickly. "Genuine Hawaiian frogs. We used to collect them by the sackful at night. Isn't that right, guys?"

It was true, so Tank and Manuel nodded.

Hurriedly Roger added, "If you shine a flashlight in their eyes, they won't move so we can catch them easily. Then we always turn them loose because none of us likes frog legs. But maybe if we helped you collect a sackful, you could take them to Kong and . . . "

Tank interrupted. "Wait a minute, Roger. I don't think . . . "

He left his thought unfinished as Josh stepped out on the lanai and called. "Hey, Tank! Come here! Hurry!"

Josh was still talking on the telephone when Tank puffed up the stairs to the Ladds' second-story apartment.

"What's up?" Tank asked.

Josh placed his hand across the mouthpiece. "Just a second." He removed his hand and spoke into the phone. "Tank is here now, so don't worry. We'll watch for your friend. Okay, Dad. See you in a little while."

Josh replaced the receiver and explained to Tank, "Dad got a call that an old friend of his named Mr. Penley has just landed at the Honolulu airport. He wants to see Dad, but he's tied up with a business appointment, so he told this man to take a cab here. Mom has to run out to shop for some things, and my sister's at a friend's place, so I've got to visit with this guy until Dad gets here."

"And you want me here in case the guy is boring," Tank guessed. "Right?"

Josh nodded as his mother rushed by, purse in hand, heading out the door.

Tank asked, "Who is this Mr. Penley?"

"He used to teach with Dad in the San Fernando Valley. I wonder why he didn't even call Dad until he had already landed at Honolulu."

"Who knows?" Tank replied. "Anyway, there's nothing to do about it now."

"I guess so." Josh walked to the sliding screen door and stepped out onto the small lanai. "We'd better stay out here where we can watch for his cab."

Tank followed Josh, who had turned to his left. His mother was already far down the street, hurrying to the little store on the corner. Closer by, Roger and Manuel were just walking away from Diz. He headed toward the Gilhooleys' apartment.

"Look at those two," Josh said, pointing at Roger and Manuel. "They look as though they're about to burst out laughing."

"They probably are, but don't dare until Diz can't hear them."

"I hope they're not going to get Diz in any trouble," Josh mused.

"They do seem awfully cheerful, considering that Diz promised Kalani that we'd all help get her surfboard back by tonight."

"Diz shouldn't have done that." Josh watched Diz knock on the Gilhooleys' apartment door. "I wonder why he's going to Kalani's place again?"

"I can't even guess." Tank leaned over the rail as a group of kids from various apartments dashed out from under a carport toward Diz.

When Kalani opened her door, the kids began chanting, "Diz's got a girlfriend. Diz's got a girlfriend."

Disaster Davis lowered his eyes, although Kalani continued to look at him with a big smile. Diz whirled suddenly and motioned to the kids. "Go away!" he yelled.

They kept coming, chanting their singsong line, "Diz's got a girl-friend."

Diz took a quick step toward them, waving his hands harder. Suddenly, his legs slipped backward from under him. A skateboard shot out from the lanai into the street just before Diz, with flailing arms, crashed ignominiously into the lanai railing.

It hit him near the waist and doubled him up like a jackknife. He fell headfirst over the lanai railing into the trunk of a 20-foot-tall rubber tree planted next to the apartment building.

Josh exclaimed, "Let's see if he's hurt."

The two boys pushed through the gang of kids who surrounded the hapless Diz, laughing and pointing at him and the skateboard that had been his undoing.

Diz was sitting up by the trunk of the rubber tree. He looked up with a silly grin at Kalani, who had run to him. She bent over him, gently examining the most recent of the many cuts and scrapes on his freckled forehead.

Josh and Tank knelt before Diz. "You okay?" Josh asked anxiously as the gang of kids quieted down and pressed close to see.

"Oh, sure." Diz waved the thought away. "I was just starting to tell Kalani what good friends Roger and Manuel are," Diz explained. "I was telling her about a plan Roger had when I accidentally stepped on that old skateboard."

Satisfied that Diz was okay, Josh gently urged the gang of kids to go play. They left, still chanting. Diz got to his feet, bashfully thanked Kalani, and followed Josh and Tank away from the apartment building.

"You have got to be more careful," Josh warned as the boys walked along the oleanders and be-still trees which hid a high chain-link fence on the other side of the roadway. "If you go back to your parents with any more cuts and scrapes, they'll never let you come here again."

Tank whispered fervently, "Yes! Yes!"

Diz didn't seem to hear. He glanced up at the sky as a beautiful white cumulus cloud drifted overhead. "Is it going to rain?" he asked.

"Might," Josh answered. "It doesn't matter if it does. It often rains in Hawaii, but people don't even wear raincoats. For one thing, they would be too hot."

"Yeah," Tank agreed. "You should be in downtown Honolulu when the secretaries and other young women are heading for work in the rain. They take off their shoes and go barefooted to the office."

"You're kidding!" Diz exclaimed.

"No, I'm not," Tank assured him just as a taxi turned into the cul-de-sac and headed up toward the apartments. "Josh, that must be your dad's friend."

A few minutes later, Josh, Tank, and Diz had introduced themselves to Doyle Penley and carried his bags upstairs to the Ladds' apartment. Mr. Penley was just under six feet tall, solidly built with bulging biceps and an old-fashioned brush haircut that suggested a military background.

Stretching out his stocking feet from where he sat in a wicker chair facing a view of Diamond Head through the lanai screen door, he said, "So Josh, how do you like living in Hawaii?"

"It's great," Josh replied, returning from the kitchen with four cans of cold drinks on a bamboo tray. "Except it's strange, being a minority for the first time in our lives."

"Minority?" the guest repeated, taking the can Josh offered.

"Yes. Tank and I are the only Caucasians in our class, but we're getting used to it."

Diz took a can from the tray and popped the top. "I go to a military academy in California, but I'd like to live here."

Josh saw Tank roll his eyes upward in a way that indicated he was grateful that Diz wasn't a permanent resident. Diz didn't seem to notice. He walked to the lanai door as a light rain began to fall.

Josh gave Tank a drink, then took the last one, set the tray on the coffee table, and sat down facing the visitor. An awkward silence began to build.

However, Josh was equal to the problem. He took a sip of his drink, then commented, "Dad said you and he used to teach together."

"Yes, for about five years, I guess. Then I got burned out and left the profession."

"What do you do now?"

"I'm an investigator with a special unit assigned to electronic company thefts in Silicon Valley. That's south of San Francisco."

"I've been there," Josh said, then repeated, "Electronic company thefts? I never heard of anything like that."

"Yeah," Tank asked, "are you like a detective?"

Penley took a sip before answering. "You've got it."

"A detective?" Diz leaned forward from where he was sitting on the rattan carpet with his back against the sofa where the guest was seated. "Are you working on a case over here?"

When Penley nodded, Tank asked, "What kind of a case?"

Penley hesitated, so Josh spoke quickly. "I don't suppose you're allowed to talk about it?"

"I can tell you a little," the investigator answered. "There have been some thefts of millions of dollars' worth of computer chips in

California. I'm trying to learn what happened to them."

"Computer chips?" Tank repeated. "I've seen pictures of them. Some are so small they'll fit on the end of my thumb, so why would anyone steal anything so little?"

"It's not the size that's important," Penley explained. "It's the information they each can store."

"Oh, of course," Tank exclaimed.

Josh said, "I've read a little about them. I believe a little tiny chip can hold up to something like four million pieces of information. Is that right?"

"That's right, Josh. But I'm sorry that's all I can say," Penley replied. "Now, tell me what you like best about Hawaii."

Josh was disappointed that the conversation had to shift, but he understood that some things were confidential. So he and Tank talked about all the exciting things they were able to do. The time went quickly, and soon Josh heard his father's station wagon pull into the carport.

While the men talked, Josh and Tank went downstairs to sit on the Catletts' first-floor lanai. Diz was standing near the oleanders, talking with Roger and Manuel.

Josh said, "I guess they're trying to think of ways to help Diz get Kalani's surfboard back."

"Could be," Tank answered.

"I guess we should be doing the same thing."

"I don't see it that way," Tank replied. "Diz got himself into that spot, so he can get himself out."

"But he told Kalani that we'd help."

"Yes, but he didn't ask my permission, or yours. So I'm not going to be concerned."

"I just don't want Diz to do something that'll make things worse with Kong." Josh snapped his fingers. "Mr. Penley is a detective. Maybe we should ask him about the strange things that have been happening on Molokai. Like the night we saw those vanishing lights."

"Yeah. That's one mystery we might solve if we can get back to Molokai." Tank paused, then continued. "But Mr. Penley's busy with his own investigation. We probably shouldn't bother him."

"You're right, so we'll just have to find a way to figure out the Molokai things by ourselves."

Josh's mother leaned over the second-story lanai and called him for dinner. He walked up the stairs, feeling excited about what might happen when they returned to Molokai.

Then he thought of Diz's promise about getting Kalani's board back tonight, and Josh shook his head.

There's no logical way that can happen, he told himself, *but knowing Diz . . .* Josh left the thought unfinished as an uncomfortable knot formed in the pit of his stomach.

Chapter Nine

A SACKFUL OF TOADS

Josh had just finished washing up for dinner when the telephone rang. He picked it up. "Hello."

"Hi, Josh, this is Diz," he heard. "I'm up at Roger's apartment on the third floor. His parents invited me to have dinner with them. They're going to serve Japanese dishes I've never tasted, like sashimi* and tofu.* They're having tacos, Roger says. So is it okay if I eat with them?"

Josh assured Diz that it was all right. After Josh replaced the receiver, he stood frowning. "Japanese dishes and Mexican tacos? Doesn't sound . . . oh! He means tako!*" Josh started to call back, then smiled. *No,* he thought, *let Diz find out that tako means octopus.*

After dinner, Josh's father and mother had driven Mr. Penley downtown to his Honolulu hotel. Josh went back to Tank's apartment moments after seeing Disaster Davis walking across the cul-de-sac with Roger and Manuel.

Josh said to Tank, "Diz had dinner with Roger's family," and told about Diz mistaking tacos for tako.

Tank laughed. "I wish I could have talked to him before he ate any. I'd have told him something to scare him, like maybe that those little suckers on the tako legs can grab on to your insides and . . . "

"Stop it!" Josh said with a grin. "The idea of eating tako would have been bad enough without you making up things. Octopus is good, but a little chewy."

"I'd rather eat rubber bands. They taste better."

"We shouldn't be sitting here like this. Instead, we should find out what plan Diz, Roger, and Manuel cooked up to get Kalani's board back tonight."

"I'm afraid to ask," Tank replied. "Anyway, those three are headed down toward Manuel's house, so let's just sit here for a while."

Josh and Tank stretched out in lounge chairs on the Catletts' lanai and looked up at Diamond Head looming above them.

"Going to rain again," Tank mused, squinting at the clouds drifting across the moon's face.

"Looks that way," Josh answered absently. Then he added, "I've been thinking about those lights on Molokai."

"Yeah? Any ideas?"

"Not really, except I'm sure the people are not night walkers, which don't exist, even if Victor seems to think they do." Josh paused, then continued thoughtfully. "Molokai is a most unusual island. It's only thirty-seven miles long and ten wide. At least half of its population are either Hawaiians or part-Hawaiians, and not too many tourists go there."

"You've been reading up on that, haven't you?"

"I guess it's what living with a former history teacher makes you do. Anyway, I can see why there are a lot of legends. For example, the ancient Hawaiians believed that great sorcerers lived there, whose reputation was so strong that for centuries the other islanders' warriors, like from Oahu* and Maui, never even tried invading Molokai."

"You're kidding? Just because the warriors were afraid of the *kahunas*?*"

"Hard to believe," Josh replied. "But true. Warriors brave enough to die in battle were scared of what they believed about some of Molokai's people. So it's understandable that some islanders would still believe in menehunes and night walkers."

"Are you thinking that maybe whoever is trying to scare us away from the heiau is responsible for those strange lights? Like maybe somebody is using them to keep people away from that area?"

"It's possible, because there has to be a logical explanation, although I can't yet figure out what it is. But beyond where Victor lives, the road is narrow and winding and rough and quiet, so it doesn't get a lot of traffic anyway."

"That's true, but it sure has some great views."

"On the other hand, Victor told us there are lots of places back on the mauka* side that are hidden from the road. People drive by without ever knowing they're there."

"Like the heiau and the lava tube we found?"

Josh nodded, started to say something, then hesitated, watching some younger boys gathering under the carport.

"What're they up to now?" Josh wondered aloud. "They're giggling and poking each other with their elbows as they did when they were teasing Diz about having a girlfriend. But he's not in sight."

"Let's find out," Tank replied. "Then let's find Diz and ask how he enjoyed his first Japanese-American food."

Josh and Tank left the lanai and started walking toward the group of boys.

Tank commented, "Seeing those kids reminds me of how the movie theaters always smell at a Saturday matinee here."

Josh wrinkled his nose. "Took me a long time to get used to the smell of dried cuttlefish being eaten instead of popcorn. My dad still says it turns his stomach, so he won't go into a theater on Saturday. I have to watch the time and come outside to meet him."

"But, like everything else that's different over here, we got used to cuttlefish. Now I even eat squid."

"It'll still never replace popcorn and candy, either in taste or smell," Josh replied.

"Neither will rice replace potatoes at every meal, but I'm getting so I can eat rice, even with chopsticks."

The friends had nearly caught up with the younger boys. Josh raised his voice to call. "Hey, what's going on?"

"Haven't you heard?" a grinning boy of about ten replied. "Roger and Manuel have taken Diz to catch toads."

"Oh," Josh replied, losing interest. He and Tank had done that many times, filling a paper sack with the harmless creatures and then letting them go.

"Then," the boy added, trying to suppress a laugh, "we're all going to hide and watch while Diz gives them to King Kong."

"What?" Josh cried. "No! They wouldn't do that!"

"They might," Tank answered solemnly. "I heard Roger say something about that this afternoon. I should have told you, but I forgot."

"I suppose they are pretty annoyed with Diz."

Tank added, "I also think they're a little bit unhappy because Kalani keeps giving Diz big smiles while almost ignoring Roger and Manuel."

"Whatever their reason, that's a mean thing to do," Josh exclaimed, "so we've got to stop them."

He pushed through the boys, starting to run down the street toward Manuel's house. Tank ran alongside of Josh.

Behind them, the younger boys shouted, "Don't mess it up! We want to see what happens when Diz hands Kong a sackful of toads!"

"I know what'll happen," Josh grimly told Tank, "and it'll be my fault! I shouldn't have let Diz out of my sight. Hurry up, Tank! We have to get there in time!"

The rain started as the friends passed the last of the oleanders and be-still trees at the end of their cul-de-sac. There they turned mauka, following the sidewalk along the left side of Diamond Head. Josh and Tank ignored the pleasant warm showers, as did the gang of younger boys trailing them.

King Kong lived with his mother at the end of a narrow street that ran back to the right, away from the road. The trade winds rustled the banana plant leaves as the boys ran by, silent now except for panting. The sweet fragrance of plumeria blossoms filled Josh's nostrils as he and Tank passed a large royal palm tree.* The Kong house came into view.

"Pst!" Someone called from the shelter of a plumeria tree. "It's Manuel!"

"And Roger," a second voice added as Josh and Tank stopped. "Don't go up there! You'll mess things up!"

"You guys shouldn't have done that," Josh said in disapproval. "Come on, Tank. Maybe we can stop Diz."

They ran on toward the Kong's house. It was board and batten* construction, once painted green but now weathered to a kind of gray. Light from the neighbor's front porch reflected off the Kong's corrugated sheet roofing, which had rusted with the rains.

The front lanai light snapped on at Kong's home. Through the light rain, Josh could see a papaya* tree with clusters of fruit just to the right of the lanai. Diz stood in front of the door, a large grocery sack clutched in both hands.

"Too late!" Tank groaned. "He's already knocked, because the light just came on."

"Let's hope it's Kong's mom . . . ," Josh started to say as the door opened. "No!"

Kong stood there, dressed only in baggy khaki shorts. He was so big that he almost filled the old screen door as he pushed it open and stepped out to face the uninvited visitor.

Diz's voice came faintly to Josh. "Kong, I brought you a present in exchange for that surfboard . . . "

"Wait, Diz!" Josh yelled, puffing from his run.

The rain suddenly started falling harder, as is common in Hawaii. Neither Diz nor Kong seemed to hear Josh above the rain. He watched helplessly as Diz shoved a rain-soaked sack toward Kong.

At the same moment, the bag burst. Toads seemed to explode from it.

Kong leaped backward, falling through the screen door, which collapsed under his great bulk. Kong sprawled on the lanai, framed by the broken door.

Diz stooped and started trying to catch the toads, which were hopping heavily away in all directions.

"Diz!" Josh yelled, hoping he could be heard above the delighted laughter of the younger boys. "Run, Diz!"

Disaster Davis looked around in confusion. He glanced first at Josh and Tank, who were frantically motioning for him to come to them. Then Diz glanced at Kong, whose backside was stuck in the screen door's frame. But Kong's voice wasn't stuck. It erupted from him in such loud, angry words that it seemed the clusters of papaya fruit would be blown from the tree.

"You pupule Mainland malihini!" Kong roared, angrily trying to break free of the wrecked screen door firmly encircling his large backside. "Kong fix you good! You wish you nevah borned!"

"Well," Diz said in a hurt tone, "if you're going to act that way when I tried to bring you a gift, I guess I'll be going."

Diz turned away as Kong struggled to his feet, the screen door still clinging to him. Kong started running, reaching out huge hands to grab Diz from behind, but the bottom of the screen door caught on the lanai post, throwing Kong off balance.

He toppled off the lanai and landed face first on the dirt and one plump toad which was still trying to escape. Kong reared up with a wild squeal and frantically wiped his mouth with a huge hand.

Josh breathed a sigh of relief as Diz continued walking haughtily away in the rain while Kong sputtered and yelled threats.

Uproarious laughter from Roger, Manuel, and the younger boys made Diz stop. A half grin on his face showed from the neighbor's front lanai light.

Josh realized that Diz still didn't understand that he was the victim of a dangerous prank. Josh dashed forward, grabbed Diz by the wrist, and started pulling him down the street. Tank ran alongside, urging, "Run, Diz! Run while we've got a chance, or we're all dead!"

As the boys distanced themselves from Kong, his voice followed them. "Kong see you othah haole boys! Josh, Tank! Kong know whe'h you live! But you not live der long, yeah?"

Kong's threat echoed in Josh's mind later that night as they sat on the Ladds' lanai and anxiously watched the street, fearful that they would see Kong coming for them.

"I'm sorry," Diz said for the umpteenth time. "I thought Roger and Manuel were my friends. I never dreamed they'd play such a mean trick on me."

"They already told us that they didn't think it would turn out this way," Josh reminded Diz.

"It isn't just you that Kong's after," Tank muttered. "He's going to watch for Josh and me too. If he catches either of us alone . . . " Tank didn't finish, but shuddered and stared down the darkened street again.

"That's certainly bad enough," Josh agreed, "but the worst part is that now Kong will never give back that board, and Kalani's father is due home in just four days."

Diz took a long, slow breath. "Well, things sure look bad, and I'm really sorry that Kong will be after you two. But I got us into this, so I'll get us out."

"No, please!" Tank pleaded, clasping his hands in mock terror. "Don't help!"

Diz looked hurt, but he sighed and replied, "Okay, I was fooled on the toads and frogs, but I promised Kalani to get her board back, so I'm going to keep trying."

For Diz's sake, Josh wished that his friend's flight home was tomorrow, but he would not fly home until the day before Mr. Gilhooley returned.

"Tank and I will try to help work something out," Josh said, but without conviction.

Tank said under his breath, "I just hope it's before Kong has used his black gloves to pound us all to pulp."

Chapter Ten

DISASTER AT CHURCH

Josh said goodnight to Tank and climbed to the second-floor apartment. His father was sitting in his easy chair, reading the newspaper. "Dad," Josh said, "I need to talk to you."

Mr. Ladd laid his paper down, removed his silver-frame half
glasses and asked, "About Detective Penley?"

"No, not that, although I'm curious." Then Josh told his father
again about vanishing lights and the bald stranger on Molokai. Josh
concluded, "I don't think there's any real danger, that he's just trying
to scare us, but I thought you should know."

His father frowned thoughtfully, glancing at the clock on top of the
television set. "It's too late to call Victor's mother, but I'll do that first
thing tomorrow. We'll find out if she phoned the police again, and
what they learned, if anything."

"Thanks, Dad." Feeling better, Josh went down the hallway to the
bedroom that he shared with his ten-year-old brother and Diz. Josh
could hear Nathan snoring softly in the bottom bunk. Diz breathed
evenly on a rollaway bed. Josh was glad that Diz could sleep, because
he had suffered a difficult and humiliating evening that ended in the

failure to get Kalani's board back. Josh didn't feel like talking about any of that, so he undressed quietly in the darkness and climbed into the top bunk. He closed his eyes and said a silent prayer, then tried to sleep. But he couldn't.

In his mind's eye, he saw again the scene with Diz and Kong over the toads. Josh thought, *That's going to make it humanly impossible to recover Kalani's surfboard before her father returns. I can't really blame Diz. He meant well. But then, he always does.*

Josh silently scolded himself. *Diz is really a nice guy, but he sure does seem to attract trouble.* Josh's thoughts flashed to the bald stranger. *What's going on over there?* There was no answer, so Josh consoled himself. *Tomorrow's Sunday. It should be a quiet, peaceful day. Then only a few more days after that, and Diz goes home. I hope he's still in one piece—and us, too.*

Reassured, Josh closed his eyes and slept.

The morning broke bright and clear with the warm trade winds blowing. Diz stirred sleepily, but little Nathan slept on. Josh pulled on a light robe and stepped into the hallway as his father was walking toward the living room.

"Oh, son," he said, "I'm glad you're up. I just called Mrs. Aka. She said the police investigated that lava tube with the padlock on the door. It's on private property, and no laws have been broken, so the authorities can't do anything."

"But what about the two fishing spears fired at us?"

"The police are investigating that, but Victor's mother told me she had the impression that the police really didn't expect to find anything more."

"So we still don't know anything, huh, Dad?"

"We know that you boys should stay away from there."

Josh thought of the heiau stones Disaster Davis still had. Josh hadn't told his father about them and didn't think it would serve any purpose to tell him now. Mr. Ladd urged Josh to wake the other two boys, then have breakfast and get ready for church.

Nathan wanted to be first in the bathroom, so he dashed down the hallway while Josh sat on the chair in front of his desk.

Diz yawned and sat up in bed. "You think Kong's still mad, Josh?"

"I'm sure of it."

"Too bad." Diz swung his long skinny legs over the side of the bed. "And all because of that surfboard thing. What do you think we should do?"

"The best thing is to stay out of Kong's way. Give him a chance to cool off. Right now, we've all got to dress, have breakfast, and leave for Sunday school."

Josh had a hard time convincing Diz that he didn't have to wear the suit his parents had insisted he take to the islands.

Mrs. Ladd tried to make Diz feel more comfortable by recalling that when they first attended church in Honolulu, she used to insist that Nathan wear a lightweight suit and shoes, like her husband. But they had developed the "Aloha spirit," she concluded, and the attitude of worship was more important than the clothes they wore.

Diz dressed for Sunday school as Josh and Nathan did, barefooted and hatless, wearing long summer-weight pants and colorful aloha shirts.* Mr. Ladd was similarly dressed, except he wore shoes. His wife and fourteen-year-old daughter wore cotton dresses. They all went downstairs to the carport.

At the church Mr. Ladd parked the station wagon in the parking lot, where the family and Diz piled out. It was a beautiful spot in a pocket valley with ancient volcanic mountains on three sides less than half a mile from the church. The valley opened on to the ocean only two hundred yards to the front.

Mr. Ladd suggested Josh introduce Diz to Dr. Chin, the Korean-born pastor with the Chinese-sounding name, so the boys walked past royal palm trees, and neat rows of red and yellow hibiscus* bushes that lined the walk from the parking lot to the church. Diz started walking backward, looking in awe at the explosion of flower colors on shrubs and trees scattered in every direction around the church.

"Over there," Josh said, also turning around and walking backward, "you see all colors of bougainvillea,* red, purple, coral and white . . . "

"Oops, sorry!" Diz exclaimed, causing Josh to look around in alarm.

A slender, middle-aged woman sprawled in a pink hibiscus bush. Her pale yellow hat had fallen over her face when Diz bumped into her.

"Here," Diz said, reaching long arms out to the woman, "let me help you."

Their efforts caused the woman to lose her hat completely. It tumbled to the lawn, giving Josh his first look at the woman. She was pretty, with dark brown eyes, light brown skin, and night-black hair just getting a few gray strands. Josh guessed she was of part Hawaiian and part Chinese ancestry.

"Thank you, boys," she said as Josh and Diz took her arms and helped her to her feet.

"I'm sorry," Diz apologized. "I didn't mean to bump . . . "

"Mom!" A girl's voice interrupted. "Are you okay?"

Josh turned to see Kalani rushing up, concern showing in her eyes.

"I'm all right," Mrs. Gilhooley said, brushing herself off while Josh retrieved her hat.

Diz slapped his open palm against his forehead. "Oh, no! Now I've done it for sure!"

Kalani, satisfied that her mother wasn't injured, introduced her to Diz.

Replacing her hat, Mrs. Gilhooley asked, "Are you the young man who borrowed my husband's prize surfboard and had it stolen?"

Diz nodded. "Yes, but it wasn't exactly stolen. And I'm going to get it back."

"Of course you are," Kalani's mother replied. "Otherwise, my daughter will be in serious trouble when her father returns."

By then, the rest of the Ladd family and several other church members had arrived. Mrs. Ladd approached and introduced herself to Mrs. Gilhooley, giving Josh and Diz an opportunity to slip away.

Diz turned around to look back, but Josh grabbed him by the shoulders and spun him around. "Watch where you're going."

"I was just looking at Kalani. She didn't smile at me just now."

"Can you blame her? Come on, and watch your step. We don't want any more accidents."

The boys walked past the church's white concrete block walls, which didn't go all the way up. The wall went up about eight feet and then there was four feet of open area above that. Josh explained that it was the way the interior was kept cool without air conditioning. So far, they had never been burglarized.

Josh introduced Diz to Dr. Chin, then steered the guest down the outside church wall to the Sunday school class. They were the first ones in, so Josh took a seat in a folding metal chair by the window and motioned for Diz to do the same next to him. A minute later, several other students arrived, including Tank. He plopped himself down next to Josh with Diz on the outside.

Tank leaned over to Josh to whisper. "We were just leaving the house when Dad got a business call from the Mainland, so we're late. Have you been thinking that it's almost time for Diz to go home?"

Before Josh could answer, a man in a pale blue suit entered. Josh recognized him as Mr. Harakawa, one of the church elders. He explained, "Your regular teacher is ill, so I'll substitute for him. As soon as everyone has settled down, we will open with prayer."

When that was finished, Mr. Harakawa announced, "Today, we will study the Golden Rule. Who knows what that is?"

Josh started to raise his hand when the door opened and Kalani Gilhooley entered. She stopped and looked around shyly at the crowded room, then at the teacher.

She said softly, "I was told that I would be in this class."

"Oh, boy!" Diz whispered, giving Josh a big smile.

Josh whispered back, "I should have realized that and invited her while we were outside. Oh, well."

Mr. Harakawa invited Kalani in, asked her name and where she was from.

"I am Kalani Gilhooley, recently from Haleiwa," she said, her voice soft and melodious. "I know Daniel," she said, smiling at Diz, "and I've met these other two boys."

Tank muttered under his breath, "She knows Daniel, but she's only met you and me."

Josh gave his friend a warning look, and Tank fell silent.

The teacher said, "We will need an extra chair. There are some stacked against the back wall. Would one of you young gentlemen . . . ?"

"I will," Diz exclaimed, starting to leap up.

Josh grabbed him by the arm. "You'd better let someone else do that," Josh said quietly. "We've had enough excitement for one day." When another boy in back had placed a chair for Kalani, Mr. Harakawa began again. "We were about to discuss the Golden Rule. Can anyone tell me what that is?"

"Yeah," Tank mumbled, "do to others before they do it to you."

"That's not funny, Tank!" Josh whispered, discreetly jabbing his elbow into his friend's ribs.

"Oh, Tank," Mr. Harakawa said, "I believe that I heard you give the answer, but some of the rest—like our visitor—might not have heard you. Repeat, please."

Tank squirmed and glanced imploringly at Josh, who shrugged and suppressed a smile.

"Well, Tank?" the teacher prompted.

"Uh . . . I . . . forgot," Tank stammered.

"I know it," Diz said, raising his hand. "'And just as you want men to treat you, treat them in the same way.' Luke 6:31."

"Very good, Daniel."

Diz lowered his eyes at the praise, but Josh saw him steal a glance at Kalani.

Apparently Tank saw it, too, for he whispered to Josh, "He'd better get that surfboard back or her father will be very angry, really huhu. But that's nothing compared to what Kong's going to do if he catches Diz alone. Serves him right, too."

Josh whispered, "Didn't you hear what the lesson verse said?"

"This is different! Diz got us in trouble with Kong, too."

"Shh! Just listen," Josh answered, and concentrated on Mr. Harakawa's application of the Golden Rule.

After everyone stood for the benediction and the class was dismissed, a couple of girls who regularly attended came to Kalani and began talking. The three boys walked out, heading for the coffee and punch table in the courtyard between Sunday school and church.

After Josh and Tank got a paper cup of punch, Josh repeated what Mr. Ladd had said about his call to Molokai.

Josh thought that Diz should have been listening attentively, but his eyes were on Kalani as she and the two girls approached the punch table.

"Uh, excuse me, fellows," Diz said, and hurriedly left them.

Josh and Tank followed him with their eyes. He went directly to the punch bowl and used the dipper to scoop some into a paper cup. He whirled around just as Kalani and the two girls came up behind him.

"Whoops!" he cried, loudly enough for Josh to hear.

In the same instant, Diz tried to pull the full cup back so it wouldn't spill on the girls. He backed into the punch table, which struck him in the back of the legs. He started to crumple, dropped the cup which splattered everywhere, and tried to regain his balance.

It was too late. Diz fell onto the punch table, which collapsed with a crash. Everyone scattered as the glass bowl sailed through the air, trailing punch. Kalani, backing away, shrieked as some of it splattered on her. The bowl landed on Diz's head, the remaining liquid pouring down over his face and ears.

"Now he's done it for sure," Tank said with grim satisfaction. "She'll never speak to him again."

Josh hurried toward the mess with Tank close behind.

Diz was extricated, unhurt but embarrassed and dripping with sticky punch. Some of the church women hastily grabbed napkins and began wiping Kalani's hands and the front of her dress.

In the confusion, with everyone trying to help Diz and Kalani, Tank whispered to Josh, "You know, I can't wait for Disaster Davis to go home."

Josh was tempted to say, "Me, too." Instead, he said, "Both Diz and Kalani will have to return to the apartments to change. I'll go get my Dad to drive. I'd better ask Kalani if she wants to ride with us."

"Us?" Tank protested. "I'm not going with you! Kong's going to be waiting!"

"Yes, I suppose he will."

"Kong's not looking for you and me. It's really Diz he wants for dumping those toads on him. So I'm going to stay here in church where it's safe."

"All right," Josh replied with disappointment in his voice. He turned to see that Diz was trying to apologize to Kalani as the women led her away.

Josh sighed. *Things are going from bad to worse,* he thought, *and the day's not even half over. What else can happen?*

It didn't take long to find out.

Chapter Eleven

SURPRISE ON A FERRY BOAT

U h-oh!" Josh exclaimed as his father turned the station wagon onto the cul-de-sac leading to their apartment.

When Mr. Ladd drove the station wagon home so Diz could clean up and change clothes, King Kong was waiting in the be-still trees beside the roadway.

Tank had changed his mind about staying at church. He rode in the backseat next to Josh. Diz sat on the other side, trying to keep his sticky, punch-soaked clothes away from Josh.

The three boys stared at Kong as they passed. He made no effort to hide, but stood where he could be seen.

Tank said, "He can't wait to get ahold of us."

Mr. Ladd commented from the front seat, "I think it's more than that. It's a kind of war of nerves. By letting you boys see him, Kong probably figures you'll suffer mentally until he can attack you physically."

Diz asked, "Mr. Ladd, isn't there anything you grown-ups can do about Kong?"

"We've tried," he replied. "Tank's parents and I talked to Mrs. Kong. So have school officials and the police. Before we moved here, Roger's and Manuel's folks did the same. Mrs. Kong always defends her son, refusing to believe he would do anything wrong. However, I will confront the boy about the stolen surfboard."

Josh thought, *I'm not sure Dad should do that because it might make Kong even more angry with me. But Kalani's board has to be returned somehow.*

Tank explained to Diz, "The school says they can't do anything about something that happens off the school grounds. The police just warn Kong, but nothing more."

"Like all bullies," Josh observed, "Kong's a coward. He won't pick on any of us unless we're alone."

Diz sighed heavily. "I'm sure sorry, fellows. It's all my fault. I'm trying to think how to make it right."

"Thanks, Diz," Josh said, "but I think the best thing is to stay away from Kong for a while."

"I've been considering this situation as we drove home," Mr. Ladd commented. "Josh and Tank have learned how to live with Kong around, and they know how to take care of themselves by staying together, as Roger and Manuel do."

"I'll stay with Josh and Tank," Diz assured Mr. Ladd.

"Oh, I'm sure you plan to do that," he replied. "I know you won't intentionally get into trouble, but we don't want anything to happen to you. So I'm going to do everything possible to return you safely to your family."

"Yay!" Tank muttered under his breath.

"So," Mr. Ladd continued, "I've thought of a solution. Of course, I'll talk with my wife first to see if she agrees, but I think she will. Then we'd have to check with Victor's mother to see if she's agreeable."

"Agreeable to what, Dad?" Josh asked.

"Letting you three boys visit her son for a few days. That is, if your parents will give you permission to go, Tank."

"They always do," Tank said cheerfully.

Josh twisted his head to look back where Kong waited in the bestill trees.

It would sure help if we could all go to Molokai until Kong cools down, Josh thought. *Maybe Diz can get back to the Mainland in one piece, and Tank and I might not get thumped by Kong.*

Diz didn't answer as Mr. Ladd eased the station wagon under the carport. "That would only be until the Kong boy calms down."

Diz said softly, "I can't go, Mr. Ladd."

Mr. Ladd turned off the key and turned to look over the back of the front seat. "Why not, Daniel?" he asked.

"I promised to get Kalani's surfboard back, and there are only a few days left before I have to fly back to the Mainland."

Mr. Ladd told Diz, "When Kalani's father returns, I'll explain everything so that you won't be in trouble."

"Maybe not with Mr. Gilhooley," Diz answered. "But it's Kalani I'm worried about. I promised her, so I have to get that board back. I would lose valuable time if I went to Molokai again. Thanks anyway, Mr. Ladd, but I need that time to get that board."

Tank protested, "But you can't do that by yourself, and Josh and I are going to Molokai."

"I know." Diz took a deep breath. "But I can't go."

"Look, Daniel," Mr. Ladd said patiently, "I appreciate your integrity, but in my judgment, it'll be safer for you to be away from that Kong boy for a while. So, in the interests of your safety, we will either send you to Molokai or back to your parents."

Josh was surprised to hear his father take such a firm tone.

However, Josh knew his dad well enough to know that he meant what he said.

"You can't send me back to Los Angeles," Diz said with a hint of defiance in his tone. "My parents will be off somewhere, as usual, and I can't go back to the military academy because of vacation. So there's nobody to stay with on the Mainland."

"Daniel," Mr. Ladd's voice had a distinct hardness now, "do you think I would let you or any other young person come visit us without having a way to reach your parents anytime I felt it was necessary?"

Diz didn't answer.

Mr. Ladd's voice softened. "You have to choose, Daniel. Which will it be?"

Tank whispered so softly only Josh could hear, "Go home!"

Josh gave him a warning glance, then turned to look at Diz, who said nothing while opening the rear door and exiting. Josh and Tank went out the other side.

As the doors slammed, Mrs. Gilhooley parked under her carport at the adjacent apartment building. Kalani got out, moving stiffly from the sticky punch on her hands, face, and clothes. Neither mother nor daughter looked toward the man and three boys, but went directly to the Gilhooley ground-floor apartment.

Diz said, "They're mad at me, and I can't blame them."

Tank commented, "Kalani will get over it, but I'm not so sure about her mother."

"Kalani won't get over it before I have to return home," Diz replied with a sad tone.

Josh's father led the way up the outside concrete steps. "Daniel, you haven't answered my question. Which do you choose?"

"Molokai," he replied quietly.

"Good!" Mr. Ladd reached the second floor and took out his door key. "Now I'd like you to change as quickly as possible. We have to return to the church to pick up the rest of my family."

When Mrs. Ladd returned from church, she gave her approval to the Molokai plan. She then phoned Mrs. Aka and was assured that the three boys were welcome and Victor could hardly wait for them to arrive.

Tank went downstairs to check with his parents, while Diz followed Josh to his room to begin packing.

Diz opened his suitcase on the rollaway bed.

Josh saw the two black volcanic stones on top of Diz's clothing. "Now you can return those," Josh said.

Diz reached for the stones. "I've had nothing but troubles since I found these."

Josh frowned, remembering that Disaster Davis always got in trouble long before he came to Hawaii. "You understand," Josh said, hearing the phone ring down the hallway, "that those have absolutely nothing to do with all the things that have been happening, don't you?"

"Oh, sure," Diz replied. "It's just the right thing to return them for environmental reasons."

The boys packed in silence until Josh's father knocked on Josh's door. "Come in," he said.

"I've got a little problem, son," Mr. Ladd explained. "That was a big advertiser on Maui who wants to see me first thing tomorrow at Lahaina.*"

"Does that mean you can't take us to the airport in the morning?" Josh asked, knowing that Maui was on the other side of Molokai from Oahu where the Ladds lived.

"I've thought that out. You boys and I will fly to Maui tonight and rent a car at the airport. Then we'll drive to Maalaea Bay* and spend the night. A friend has a condo there that he said I could use."

"I remember," Josh replied. "Nice place."

"He's in Japan, so we'll get the key from the manager, have dinner overlooking the ocean, and then get a good night's rest. It's only a short drive to Lahaina from there, so I'll be there in plenty of time for my appointment in the morning."

Josh visualized Maui, where he had been several times. "But the airport's at Kahului,* and that's the opposite direction from Lahaina."

"You boys won't fly to Molokai. You'll take the morning ferry from Lahaina to Kaunakakai,* where Mrs. Aka and Victor will meet you."

Josh exclaimed, "Hey, Diz, I've never taken the ferry, so it should be fun!"

Diz didn't answer, but went on glumly packing.

Mr. Ladd warned, "Sometimes it can be rough, crossing that Kalohi Channel,* but the ferry has a stabilizer to help reduce rolling, so it should be an enjoyable trip."

"Sounds good, Dad."

"Then as soon as we're all packed, we'll be on our way."

Disaster Davis was still glum and quiet when the inter-island jet landed at Kahului near Maui's northwest shore. Mr. Ladd rented a four-door sedan. The bags were loaded in the trunk. Tank and Diz sat in back. Diz turned to look out the window, still not saying anything.

Josh's father gave him the rental-agency map and motioned for him to sit up front. "You're the navigator, son," Mr. Ladd said, "so find Highway 30, and we'll take it straight south."

Josh always enjoyed maps, especially the one of Maui. The island resembled a woman's head and upper torso, with the head to the northwest. Highway 30 went straight south across the woman's neck, like a necklace. The West Maui Forest Reserve rose to the right. Vast fields of growing sugar cane on both sides of the road swayed to the strong trade winds.

"I've been intending to tell you boys something," Mr. Ladd commented as they rolled along. "Remember that detective, Penley?"

"Sure," Josh replied. "He was working on a case about some stolen computer chips."

"But he wouldn't tell us if that had anything to do with his being here in Hawaii," Tank added.

Josh looked at Diz, who had been present at the meeting with the detective. But Diz continued to stare out the window, showing no interest in the subject.

"I guess he felt that he could tell me a little about what he was working on."

"Can you tell us?" Tank asked.

"I don't see why not," Josh's father replied. "Mr. Penley said that computer chips are sent to Asia because it's what he called a 'labor-intensive market.' Part of the processing takes place there. Then the chips are either sent back to the manufacturer or directly to distributors."

"Asia," Josh mused. "Hawaii is considered the crossroads between the United States and Asia. So the chips then pass through here, going or coming. Is that by air or surface, Dad?"

"By air, Penley told me."

Josh laid the map on his lap and thought about that. He had learned to use a computer in school, but he never had any interest in the way they worked.

"We should be coming up on our turnoff pretty soon," Josh's father said. "Better check the map."

Josh did, following their progress from the airport. On the map, near the woman's chin, Highway 30 veered right and followed the coast up to the old whaling town of Lahaina.

"Highway 31 cuts over to the left just about where the woman's chin was on the map," Josh said. He looked through the windshield. "That must be it up ahead."

In a few minutes, they turned off onto a quiet road in back of a row of multistoried condos.

As they took the elevator to the third floor, Josh asked Diz, "You ever going to speak again?"

"I was just thinking," he replied. "I'm breaking my word to get Kalani's board back. She's going to be in trouble with her dad. I'd rather have Kong work me over than let that happen to her."

Josh didn't know what to say, so he looked at Tank. He shrugged and suggested they go swimming before dinner.

Josh and Tank did, but Diz sat on the small lanai and looked out toward the island of Kahoolawe* with the islet called Molokini* nearby.

"I feel terrible about Diz," Josh admitted, treading water just off the shore.

"Yeah, me too," Tank answered. "But I'll feel better when he's back on the Mainland and our lives can return to normal."

"Maybe he'll perk up when we get on the ferry tomorrow," Josh said hopefully. "Maybe we'll find a clue about those mysterious vanishing lights, and that'll give Diz something to think about besides that surfboard."

The ferry had two decks, Josh saw the next morning when he and the other two boys went aboard with a number of other people. The boys debated about whether to ride on the enclosed lower deck with its large water-stained windows, or up on the open topside where the wind would be stronger.

Josh asked, "Diz, what do you want to do?"

He answered in a miserable voice, "I'm going home in a couple of days, and you know what I want."

Tank complained, "If you don't snap out of it, you're going to ruin everything for Josh and me."

"I'm sorry, but I can't help how I feel."

"Okay," Josh said resignedly, "let's all sit down below out of the wind."

They sat on the right where they could see Lahaina as the ferry got under way. Diz lapsed back into silence, but the other boys commented about all the sights.

"Those sailboats and catamarans sure are pretty," Josh said, looking where they rode at anchor offshore.

"I like those guys parasailing," Tank remarked. "That looks like fun, being towed by a motorboat and being lifted up by parachute to float down to the water."

Josh's gaze turned shoreward. Many trees marked the old town where it sprawled along the coast. Behind the community, a treeless mountain sloped upward toward great masses of white clouds so common to the islands.

The ferry picked up speed and started to roll slightly as it left the town behind. Josh commented, "My dad told me some exciting stories about Lahaina back in the mid to late 1800s. That's when the first missionaries and sailors off the whale ships clashed over their different ideas about the native Hawaiians."

Diz stood and broke his silence. "I think I'll get some fresh air."

"If you're feeling a little queasy," Josh warned, "you'll probably feel the motion more on the top deck than you do down here."

"I'll be okay," Diz replied, heading outside where steps led to the upper deck.

Tank asked anxiously, "Do you think we dare risk letting him be up there by himself?"

"With his ability to get into trouble, maybe we should go up and stay with him."

The friends rose and headed toward the rear, swaying slightly with the ferry's gentle roll.

"Hey!" Tank exclaimed. "He's already coming back."

Josh stopped and waited for Diz. "I guess it was a little too rough up . . . " Josh didn't finish his thought.

"What's the matter?" Tank asked.

"Look at his face! He's all excited."

Josh and Tank hurried to meet Diz. His eyes were bright as he exclaimed, "Guess who's up there?"

"Who?" Josh and Tank asked together.

"The bald-headed man! The very same one!"

Chapter Twelve

WHEN TIME IS ALMOST GONE

The bald man?" Josh asked, glancing toward the upper deck. He saw only a crewman standing at the top of the steps. "You sure, Diz?"

Disaster Davis nodded vigorously. His listlessness had vanished. His face was flushed with excitement. "I tell you, it's him!"

Tank asked, "Did he see you?"

"I don't think so."

Tank suggested, "Josh, maybe we'd better take a look for ourselves."

Josh asked Diz, "Where is he?"

"Sitting well forward, on the right side."

"Well?" Tank asked impatiently. "Should we look?"

"Okay," Josh agreed, "but there's only room for one person at a time on that ladder. You want to go?"

Tank considered that for a moment. "Maybe you'd better."

Josh asked, "Are you thinking that it would be your luck to stick your head up over the last rung and see him looking straight down at you?"

"I thought of that," Tank admitted with a grin. "But I'm willing to

103

let you go first, because that's what friends are for."

Diz said sharply, "Quit kidding, you guys!"

"Okay," Josh agreed, and started up the ladder. He slowed near the top and carefully looked over the open deck. A few of the passengers were standing by the rail, their hair blown by the stiff sea breeze. Most passengers sat in long rows, facing forward. None seemed to notice Josh, and he did not see the bald man.

Josh hoisted himself onto the open top deck and immediately took the nearest seat. He wanted to be inconspicuous while locating his man.

Josh's eyes probed quickly to the rows of seats on the right and toward the front. *There!* Josh thought. *At least, it looks like him from the back. I'd better wait until he turns his head to make sure.*

Moments later, the bald man turned around and looked back. Josh's instinct was to duck, but he forced himself to lower his head slightly in order to shield his face, but not to move or turn away.

He was still able to see the man, so when he turned around to face the ferry's bow again, Josh sighed with relief and quickly rose. He started down the ladder, then glanced back for a final look.

At the same moment, the bald man twisted around, and their eyes met. The man frowned, staring at Josh. He tried to act natural by looking down at the ladder and then descending.

"Well?" Tank asked as Josh reached the lower deck.

"It's the same man," Josh replied. "He turned around and looked at me. I saw him frown, so I think he was trying to decide if he had seen me before."

Diz asked anxiously, "If he does, what'll we do?"

"Can't hide on this boat," Tank answered.

"No," Josh agreed, "but we can spread out so that if he comes down to check me out, we won't be together."

"Yeah," Tank agreed. "If he did that, and he saw Diz and me, he'd know for sure where he saw us before."

"So let's move away from each other," Diz suggested, starting back inside the enclosed deck. "If he does come down, that'll mean he's suspicious and is checking us out, but let's try to keep him from seeing us."

"Maybe this is our big break," Tank said hopefully as they stepped into the sheltered area. "If we stay out of sight until we dock, maybe we can follow him . . . No, we'll be in Mrs. Aka's car."

Diz suggested, "But if the bald guy drives away, we could get his license number."

Tank shook his head. "What good will that do? We can't just walk into a police station and ask them to tell us whose license number that is."

"Too bad we don't have a camera," Diz commented. "We could at least take his picture."

"We don't want his picture." Tank's tone held a hint of impatience and sarcasm. "We want to know who he is, where he's going, and what he's doing on Molokai. Then maybe we'll know why he chased us and fired that fish spear at us."

"Let's spread out and try to think," Josh said. "It's an hour-and-fifteen-minute ride, so if he doesn't come down in the next half hour, let's get back together and compare our plans."

Josh walked forward and sat next to the high windows on the left. They were now drenched with salt spray as the ferry hit full speed in the choppy channel. He looked back and saw that Diz was in the middle of a row mostly occupied by older women. Tank was in the right rear.

The time seemed to drag, but when several minutes had gone by and the bald man had not come walking through the lower deck, Josh breathed easier. When he judged that it had been half an hour since he was on the upper deck, Josh stood up and walked toward the stern. Tank and Diz joined him there and worked out a plan.

When the ferry slowed and eased toward the Kaunakakai Wharf, where once pineapple barges loaded at Molokai's biggest town, the boys put their plan into action. They spread out along the lower deck. Josh stationed himself near the bow. Diz took the middle, and Tank stood near the stern.

By now the big windows were so stained with drying salt spray that it was difficult for anyone outside to see through the glass. Even so, the boys tried to make themselves as inconspicuous as possible while other lower-deck passengers disembarked, mingling with those from the upper deck. That included the bald man, who didn't look back as he stepped onto the wharf, carrying scuba equipment, a black wetsuit, and a small flight bag.

Josh felt his heart speed up with excitement when another man met the bald one. They spoke briefly but didn't shake hands, suggesting to the watching boy that the men had not been apart long.

The second man took the new arrival's wet suit and flight bag and led the way off the wharf.

Josh ran toward the stern. "Come on," he cried, passing Diz and heading for Tank. "Remember our plan. I'll meet Victor and his mother. You two mingle with the crowd and try to follow close enough to see if those men get in a car. But don't let them see you."

A couple of minutes later Josh smiled and hurried up to the woman and boy waiting on the wharf. "Hi, Mrs. Aka, Victor," Josh said. "It's good to see you again."

"You, too," Victor replied with a welcoming smile.

His mother asked, "Where are your friends going?"

"They're following those two men we saw near the heiau."

"Is that who they are?" Victor asked in surprise.

"Sure are. Let's walk slowly," Josh urged, carrying his overnight bag. "I'll fill you in as we go."

By the time they reached the end of the wharf, the passengers had dispersed. Tank was standing on the dock, facing the water.

"Well?" Josh asked as he came even with Tank.

He turned around. "They climbed in an old green panel truck without any signs or anything," Tank replied. "I think it's one of those four-wheel-drive kinds. Oh, there was a driver waiting for them in the truck."

Diz rushed up, eyes bright with excitement. "I'm sure that they didn't see us." He pointed to the right. "They took off down that way, but not before we got the license number in case we need it."

"That's the way we're going," Victor said. "You want to try following them?"

"Hold on, boys," Mrs. Aka broke in with a warm smile. "First, I want to welcome you back to our island. Next, I want you to know our old car runs, but not fast. We can't chase anybody. Okay?"

They nodded and followed Victor and his mother to their sedan, all the while updating Victor on all the latest developments.

"So," Josh concluded, "things haven't been going well for any of us."

"It's worse for me," Diz added, getting into the backseat followed by Josh and Tank. "I'm taking the Red Eye* home tomorrow evening, and I haven't kept my word to Kalani about recovering her dad's surfboard. Coming over here wrecks any chance of ever doing that."

"At least you'll have some rest from Kong," Victor replied. "And maybe we'll have some fun now that we know the bald man and his friend are back on the island."

Diz did not seem consoled. He again lapsed into silence as Victor's mother headed out of Kaunakaki. Even though it was the island's biggest town, it did not have even one stoplight.

The car headed east along the main road, Highway 450, which Mrs. Aka said was more commonly known as Kamehameha V.* It followed the southern shoreline, with the mountains on the left and the ocean about two hundred yards to the right.

Josh was excited about the fact that the bald man and his companion had headed down this same road. He kept a sharp lookout for a green panel truck while Victor's mother pointed out the sights.

Diz sighed heavily, causing Josh to look around. Diz was still looking out the left window, lost in his misery. It hurt Josh to see Diz like that.

"I know you're very disappointed," Josh said, "but there's nothing you can do about Kalani's board now."

Diz whirled to face Josh. "You're not the one who's breaking a promise! You're not the one who has to fly back to California and leave Kalani thinking you're a liar!"

Josh was taken aback at Diz's angry outburst. "I'm partly to blame, remember? I said I'd help get that board back, and I will. When we return to Honolulu . . . "

"When we return," Diz snapped, "*you* can still try to get it back, but I'll be flying across the Pacific!" He turned away, looking toward the mountain again.

Josh was sorry, but he didn't know what else to say. He glanced at Tank, who shrugged.

From the front seat, Victor's mother must have overheard Diz's sharp outburst, but she didn't let on. Instead, she acted as a tour guide.

"In a few minutes," she said, "we'll be coming up on some eight-hundred-year-old fishponds that belonged to the old Hawaiian royalty, the alii.* But before that, there's St. Joseph's Church. It was built by Father Damien, the leper priest."

Josh turned to Diz, again hoping to get him to quit moping and join in the conversation. "You ever hear about Father Damien, Diz?" He didn't answer, so Josh turned back to listen to Victor's mother.

"Over there," she said, pointing to the right, "is where my grandmother's house used to stand. A tidal wave took it. Good thing she wasn't home at the time."

Josh looked at the ocean through different eyes as Mrs. Aka told what had happened. For years, as a little girl, she had played around her grandmother's home. From it, there had been a beautiful ocean view.

Then one night there had been a tsunami,* one of those great tidal waves that rise up from the sea and rush inland, a wall of powerful water twenty, forty, perhaps sixty feet high. When it returned to the sea that spawned it, it took the grandmother's house. Every shrub, plumeria tree, and hibiscus plant were also gone.

"How awful," Diz said softly.

Josh was pleased to see Disaster Davis showing some interest in anything besides his problem.

Josh wanted to say something to further encourage Diz, but Diz abruptly jabbed a forefinger across the front seat. It was so sudden that Victor, sitting beside his mother, jerked his head back.

"There's their truck!" Diz cried. "See it?"

Josh joined the others in looking through the windshield at a small beachside park where several vehicles were parked under palm trees.

"That's it, all right," Tank agreed, his voice rising with excitement. "Now what'll we do?"

"Check the license number," Diz replied.

"Don't slow down, Mrs. Aka," Josh urged as he felt the speed slacken slightly. "We don't want to make them suspicious. Drive on past. All of you try to see where those men are."

Josh's excitement rose as Mrs. Aka passed the panel truck. There were a half-dozen women and children, sitting or strolling, but no sign of the three men.

Diz exclaimed, "The license number's the same, so there's no doubt it's the right vehicle. But where are those men?"

The other boys all looked back, but each admitted he hadn't seen either the bald man or his companions.

"What'll we do?" Diz asked. "Stop and walk back?"

"What good would that do?" Josh asked.

Reluctantly, the others agreed, so the sedan continued down the road. The dry terrain gradually gave way to more lush greenery. The boys held a lively discussion about what they should do later, with brief interruptions by Victor's mother. She pointed out small homes partially hidden in little valleys and an occasional waterfall on the mountainside.

The road narrowed and sharp curves forced the car to slow as it climbed toward Halawa Valley.* "But we aren't going that far," Mrs. Aka said, glancing in the rearview mirror. "I'd better try to pull over. There's a driver behind me who's coming up awfully fast."

Josh turned to look back. He stiffened, whirling around to face front again. "Don't look now, Tank," he said with sudden excitement, "but that's the same truck!"

Tank didn't have to look back, for the truck suddenly accelerated, speeding past the slower sedan with an angry blast of the horn.

"It's them!" Tank cried.

"Sure is!" Diz agreed. "It's the same two guys from the boat, and the driver who was waiting for them."

Victor urged, "Mom, try to catch up with them."

"This old car's already giving its best. You boys will just have to forget about following them."

Josh and the others sank back in disappointment.

Josh asked, "Where do you think they're headed?"

"To the heiau," Tank guessed. "Maybe we'll see them when Diz returns those rocks."

"You boys had better stay away from there," Mrs. Aka warned.

"What?" Diz exclaimed. "I'm going home tomorrow, but first I've got to return some rocks I took from there."

"I'll have my husband do that. When I talked to Josh's father, he and I agreed that there's something very strange going on around that place. So you boys had better stay away."

That started a chorus of protests, but Victor's mother was firm. Gradually the boys quieted down and sank back into their seats in glum silence.

Josh idly glanced out the window as the Aka car passed a red pickup truck parked beside the road just a hundred yards from the ocean. Two local boys lifted surfboards from the back of the truck.

Josh sat up with a startled cry. "Look! There's Kong! And he's got Kalani's surfboard!"

Chapter Thirteen

"DISASTER DAVIS" DISAPPEARS

Diz leaned across Josh to see better out the right window. "You're right! That's Kong with Kalani's board. Mrs. Aka, please stop and let us out."

"Hold on," Josh cautioned as the old sedan slowed. "Diz, what do you think you're going to do? Walk up to Kong and take the board away from him?"

"Yeah," Tank added, "especially when he's with another kid old enough to drive that pickup."

"There are four of us boys," Diz persisted. "Oh, please! Let's stop so I can try talking to Kong! This may be our last chance, because tomorrow I fly home."

Victor's mother resumed speed. "Victor and Mr. Ladd told me about this Kong boy," she said. "I will not be responsible for you boys getting hurt. I'm sorry."

Diz slumped back with an angry huffing sound, but Josh secretly agreed with Mrs. Aka. Aloud, Josh tried to sound consoling. "I remember Kong saying some days ago that he was going to Molokai to visit a calabash cousin. Maybe he lives around here."

Victor said, "There are a few houses tucked back under the trees around here. So maybe Josh is right."

Josh turned to look back. "How about that red pickup, Victor? You ever see it before?"

After another look, Victor shook his head. "I don't think so."

"I believe that I've seen it," his mother said, looking in the rearview mirror. "There's a kind of wild young man who lives back in one of those little valleys in the mountain. First name is Walter. I don't know his last."

"I think you're right, Mom!" Victor exclaimed. "I didn't get a good look at the guy with Kong, but it could have been Walter." Victor hesitated, then added, "Some of the kids at school say he's a pakalolo* grower."

"What's that?" Diz wanted to know.

"Marijuana," Josh explained.

"Which reminds me," Mrs. Aka said, "you boys be careful tramping around back in that underbrush. It's rumored that's where some of that illegal weed is grown, and the owners won't hesitate to hurt someone who gets too close to their plants."

"Oh, Mom," Victor scoffed, "I've been playing back there for years and never seen anything like that."

"Just the same, you boys be careful."

Josh was surprised to see that Diz had perked up when they stopped at the Aka home a few minutes later. Victor led the three visitors inside, where they dropped their duffel bags in Victor's room.

"Well," he asked as Diz unzipped his bag, "what do you guys want to do first?"

"Go snorkeling," Tank replied promptly. "Diz, do you know that Hawaii's waters are about the clearest in the world, and you can see forever under there?"

"So I heard," Diz answered, straightening up with the two black volcanic stones in his hand. "But first, I want to return these to the heiau."

Josh frowned in disapproval. "You heard Mrs. Aka. Her husband will take those stones back. We're not to go near that place."

"I've thought about that," Diz answered, rolling the rough stones in his open palms, "but he might not put them back exactly where I found them. So I'm not going to take any chances."

"Sorry, Diz," Josh said firmly, "but we have to do what Victor's mom said."

Disaster Davis met Josh's steady gaze for several seconds before he shrugged. "Okay," he said, shoving the stones into his pockets. "Let's go to the beach."

Victor asked permission to borrow his mother's mask, fins, and snorkel, along with his father's. With his new equipment and an old set, there were enough for all four boys. They walked about two hundred yards across the road to the small beach. It was totally deserted, with only the sound of the trade winds in the palm fronds and the surf crashing on the shore.

The three experienced boys showed Diz how to use the combination snorkel and face mask. He imitated them in putting on fins at the water's edge.

"Remember, Diz," Josh warned, "when you're around coral, don't stick your hands in a hole, or you may get bitten by a moray eel."

Victor explained, "That's right. Many kinds of puhu kauila* live in those holes. Some are not dangerous, but you never know which one might take off a finger, like the moray eel."

"I'll be careful," Diz promised. "Oh, I'd better not take these in the water." He removed the black volcanic stones from his pockets and awkwardly walked with fins back up on the beach. "Might lose them," he explained, leaving the rocks next to the trunk of a palm.

The boys spent an enjoyable hour swimming on the surface or just under it, watching myriads of brightly colored fish darting about like fragments of a broken rainbow. Josh saw no eels, which suited him just fine.

But even as he snorkeled, Josh's mind kept drifting away, alternating between the mystery of the vanishing lights and how to recover Kalani's surfboard.

Apparently Disaster Davis was thinking about the board, too. While Tank and Victor swam in deeper water about a hundred feet away, with only the ends of their snorkels showing, Diz swam alongside Josh and raised his mask. "I've been trying to get my bearings," Diz explained. "Is that the direction to the heiau?"

Josh followed Diz's pointing arm. "Yes, but remember what Mrs. Aka said, so stay away from there."

"I've been thinking," Diz said, ignoring Josh's warning, "that we've got an unusual opportunity to get Kalani's board back. I mean, who would have guessed that Kong would be here with that board at the same time we are?"

Josh admitted, "It's pretty unusual, all right."

"Call it coincidence," Diz added, "but I think that means we should get that board back before I have to leave for California."

Josh raised his eyebrows in a questioning manner, already guessing what Diz was thinking of doing.

"Besides," Diz added, "doesn't the Bible say something like God causes all things to work together for good?"

"That's only part of the quote, Diz. The rest says ' . . . to those who are called according to His purpose.'* So I'm not sure that applies in this situation."

"Well, I'm sure it's the right thing to return Kalani's surfboard. So I'd like to find out where Kong is staying with this friend, Walter, and go talk to him."

"I wouldn't do that. You heard what Mrs. Aka said about this Walter maybe being a pakalolo grower. You could run into a booby trap or something else that would hurt you even before you got to his place."

"Then I'd like to go down to where we saw Kong and Walter with the pickup. That's not far from here, and they probably go surfing there every day. Maybe they're still there right now."

"I think we should let my father see if he can work something out with Kong's mother. After all, Kong stole that board, and I doubt that Mrs. Kong would approve of her son stealing."

"Regardless of that, I made a promise to Kalani . . . "

"I know! I know!" Josh interrupted. "I'm one hundred percent in favor of getting that board back. You and I disagree only on how best to do that."

"There's not much time left for me to make good . . . "

Diz broke off as a shriek rose above the sound of the waves and the palm trees.

Josh and Diz looked out over the water to where Tank and Victor were treading water and waving their hands excitedly.

"Something's wrong!" Josh exclaimed. "I'd better go see." He lowered his mask into place.

"Doesn't sound too serious," Diz replied. "I think I'll work on my suntan."

Josh's flippers and strong strokes quickly drove him across the intervening water to where the other two boys were swimming toward shore. Josh couldn't be sure by looking through his mask, which was constantly splashed by waves, but he thought he saw blood on the right side of Tank's face. Josh put on an extra burst of speed, swimming as fast as he could.

It was blood, Josh saw when he got closer. "What's the matter?" he asked, raising his mask as the other two boys met him.

"A little eel grabbed my ear," Tank panted, twisting his head so Josh could see. "How bad is it?"

"I can't tell because it's bleeding pretty bad."

"Ears always bleed a lot," Victor said. "I looked at it after I made the eel let go, and it didn't seem too bad."

"Let's get ashore fast," Josh said, "and make sure."

On the small strip of sand, Josh removed his mask and checked Tank's ear. "I think we'd better get Mrs. Aka's opinion," Josh said.

"That bad, huh?" Tank asked, removing his flippers with his left hand and holding his right over the ear.

"I didn't say that," Josh replied, leading the way across the sand. "But mothers always know best about these kinds of things."

"How'd it happen?" Josh asked as the boys trotted toward the monkeypod tree and the Akas' front door.

"I saw this little eel," Tank explained. "Little fellow, not even a foot long. He looked harmless, so when he swam out of his hole, I let him get too close to my face. I guess he thought my ear was something to eat, because he suddenly flashed in and bit."

"I'll say!" Victor added. "It wouldn't let go. I finally grabbed it by the back of the head like a person would a poisonous snake. Even then, it wouldn't let go until I squeezed hard."

Tank removed his right hand from his ear and gulped, looking at the bloody fingers. He asked anxiously, "You think I'm going to be okay, Josh?"

Josh took another glance as he jogged beside his friend. "I think so.

The bleeding seems to be slowing."

Victor said, "Did you know that blood looks green under these waters?"

Before either Josh or Tank could reply, Josh suddenly remembered Disaster Davis. Josh spun around.

"Where's Diz?" he asked.

The other two boys twisted their heads to look over their shoulders, but kept jogging. "Last I saw of him," Victor said, "he was sunning himself on the beach."

A stab of fear penetrated Josh's heart. He looked at Tank. "Will you be okay for a minute?"

"I'm not dying, you know," Tank replied a little sharply. "I just got a little bite on my ear."

Josh didn't mind his friend's tone because he understood that he was scared in spite of trying to sound brave. "I just want to check on where Diz went," Josh explained, breaking into a run back toward the beach.

It took him only a few seconds to reach the area where he had last seen Diz. Quickly Josh looked up and down the beach, then scanned the water's surface. His heart began to thump hard, and not just from running.

He's not in the water, Josh reasoned, *or I'd have seen him. He's not on the beach, so where . . . ?*

"Oh, I hope not!" Josh exclaimed aloud as a fearful thought hit him. "To face Kong and his friend alone—no! Diz does klutzy things, but he wouldn't do anything like that! Or would he?"

Josh started to cup his hands to call when he remembered the black stones from the heiau. He ran to the palm tree where he had last seen them.

He glanced down quickly and swallowed hard. "Gone!" Josh

breathed the word aloud.

Sprinting back to the house, Josh dashed under the immense monkeypod tree, across the front lanai and into the house. "Where is everybody?" he called.

"In the bathroom," Tank replied.

Josh said a quick silent prayer of relief.

Victor stood in the bathroom doorway. His mother and Tank were by the sink where she was just taping a bandage over his right ear. He didn't move his head, but turned his eyes toward Josh.

"Good thing that was such a little eel," Tank said with a wide grin. "I won't even need stitches."

"Thank God for that!" Josh said, returning the smile and heaving a big sigh of relief.

Victor commented, "I think the real reason that Tank didn't get hurt more was because the eel decided he didn't like the taste, but he had his teeth stuck in Tank's tough old ear and couldn't let go."

"Victor!" his mother said reprovingly, but she smiled and added, "There, Tank. That should do it."

"Thanks." Tank glanced at Josh and asked, "Where's Diz?"

"One of two places, I'm afraid," Josh answered. "Either he's gone to return those rocks to the heiau . . . "

"Or to find Kong!" Tank guessed.

"That's the way I figure it," Josh replied. He quickly told about the heiau rocks and the conversation he had with Diz a while before.

"So," Victor asked, "which do you think he did—went to find Kong, or to return those rocks?"

"It's hard to guess," Josh admitted. "But either way, he's headed for big trouble."

"And, knowing you," Tank replied grimly, "you're going to be right behind him trying to help."

"I feel responsible for him. I can't leave him out there alone, knowing that whichever place he goes, he's bound to end up in more trouble than he can handle."

Tank took a slow, deep breath. "Well, I think that whatever he did, it was downright foolish. But you can't go off alone after him." Tank turned to Victor's mother. "Do you think this ear will be okay if I go with Josh?"

"The ear isn't seriously injured," she replied thoughtfully. "But I wish you boys could wait until my husband gets home so he could go with you."

"So do I," Josh answered, "but this can't wait. Tank, you ready?"

"Let's go," he said.

"Me too, huh, Mom?" Victor glanced imploringly at his mother.

She closed her eyes for a moment, then opened them and nodded. "All right, but please be very careful."

"We will," they promised together and raced outside.

Passing under the monkeypod tree, Victor asked, "Which way do you think he went? Down the road to Kong, or up the mountain to the heiau?"

"Yeah," Tank said, "we can't afford to make a mistake. If we go to the wrong place, it may be too late."

Which way did Diz go? Josh wondered, trying to think what Diz had most likely done.

"No matter which way he went," Tank said with annoyance, "I'll bet he's already in trouble."

Josh didn't bet, but he had a feeling that Tank was right.

Victor urged, "Let's not stand here debating! Knowing how much Diz wants that surfboard back, I'd say he went to see Kong."

Chapter Fourteen

UP FROM THE OCEAN

Tank agreed. "Sounds logical to me."

Josh shook his head. "Diz would know that he'd get hurt if he went alone to face Kong. So I'd say he went to the heiau."

"Then let's go there," Tank replied.

The three boys headed that way, while Josh remembered having already been chased away from the heiau and the two fishing spears that had been fired at them.

Josh thought, *I don't like it. Diz is gone, and I think I know where. But what about that man we saw on the ferry? Suppose he's also at the heiau?*

The boys were breathing hard when they caught sight of part of the heiau straight ahead.

"Let's stop and listen," Josh suggested, panting from the exertion of climbing.

"But not for too long," Tank cautioned, "or we may be too late to help Diz."

"He may not need any help," Josh replied hopefully.

Still, when he had held his breath and listened hard without hearing anything, he wondered if he was kidding himself. *Knowing Diz*, he told himself, *he'll need help.*

The boys bent forward, keeping low, and moved as silently as possible toward the heiau. It rose before them out of the dense underbrush where it had been hidden for countless years.

Carefully, the boys climbed the wall-like side nearest them with Josh leading. He gingerly raised his head so he could see over the top. He sucked in his breath and looked down at Tank and Victor below him.

"Go back!" Josh urgently whispered.

Wordlessly, they backed down to the ground where Josh explained what he had seen. "They've got Diz tied up with his mouth taped."

"Who has?" Tank whispered back.

"The bald man and two others."

"The ones in the green truck," Victor guessed in a low voice.

"What'll we do now?" Tank wanted to know.

Josh thought fast. "Distract them."

"Huh?" Victor asked.

"You know," Josh replied, keeping his voice low. "Some of us let the men see us, and we run. We lead them away while the other person frees Diz. Then we all meet back at the house where Victor's mother can call the police."

"What happens if we get caught?" Tank's voice had a hint of a waver in it as though he were getting scared. "Or they start in with that sling gun again? Can't outrun one of those fish spears."

"Mustn't let that happen," Josh said firmly. "Now, anybody got a preference as to which they want to do?"

Nobody volunteered, so Josh decided. "I'm a fairly fast runner, so I'll be the decoy. You two free Diz when I lead those men far enough away."

Tank asked, "What happens if they don't all chase you, but some stay with Diz?"

"Then one of you decoy him away while the other helps Diz. Anybody got a knife to cut his ropes?"

"I have." Victor patted his right front pocket.

"Then you free him. Tank, you may have to be the second decoy."

"Oh, fine!" he answered with a groan. "I just hope I don't end up as lifeless as a real decoy."

"I don't think those men really want to hurt anybody," Josh said, trying to sound confident. "They just want to scare us away."

"Well, that's sure working on me!" Tank admitted.

"That'll help you run faster," Josh replied, forcing a smile. "Okay, let's listen closely. Here's what I think we should do."

He pointed out the way he planned to go and indicated the approach Tank and Victor should take across the open heiau, approaching Diz from behind. When Josh finished, he asked, "Either of you have a better idea?"

When neither did, Josh turned and circled around the heiau, planning to come up facing the men on the other side of the structure. As he slipped up to the last corner, his heart was thudding so hard that he was afraid the men would hear it.

Holding his breath, Josh peered around the corner. *The truck!* It was parked in the midst of many small trees, the back end toward the low part of the heiau. The front faced down the mountain. The vehicle stood high off the ground, confirming Josh's earlier thought that is was an off-road, four-wheel-drive vehicle.

Josh asked himself, *But what's it doing up here?* Then he knew. *I was right. They're into some kind of illegal activity, and they need the panel truck. But . . . what kind of activity are they in? No time to think about that. Got to free Diz.*

Josh looked around and chose the route he planned to take when he was pursued. Taking a deep breath, he started to stand up where the men could see him. *No, wait!* he told himself, glancing back at the truck. *I have a better idea.*

Keeping low to the ground, trying to keep from breathing so loudly that he could be heard, Josh ignored his thumping heart and approached the panel truck. He first peered through the driver's side window to make sure nobody was there, then he opened the door.

It squeaked so loudly that Josh froze, adrenalin pulsing through his veins. When the men didn't come to the edge of the heiau to investigate, Josh carefully raised up to peer over the top of the truck. *They're still standing around Diz. Must not have heard me.*

He risked peering over the front seat into the open back of the panel vehicle. *Boxes of something. And a small suitcase. Can't tell what's in them. Well, stop looking and act, Josh!*

He was still too young to drive, but he knew about the brakes and gear shifts. *Lord, I sure hope I'm doing the right thing, but it's the only way I know to save Diz.*

Josh reached inside and put the truck in neutral, then he released the hand brake. The vehicle lurched forward so suddenly that Josh was almost thrown off balance. He recovered quickly and raced for the shelter of the nearest tree trunk while the truck gained speed, breaking down small shrubs and smashing through brush like a runaway boulder.

"Hey!" one of the men shouted from the heiau and ran to where Josh could see him. "The truck! Baldy, you crazy idiot! You didn't set the brake right!"

"I'm sure I did, but never mind that now!" the bald man cried, hurrying down the low side of the heiau. "We've got to stop it!"

Josh watched with satisfaction as all three men ran wildly down the hill after the green panel truck. It struck an ancient volcanic outcropping and bounced high. One side of the rear door flew open and a small bag sailed through the air. It landed and started to roll downhill but was stopped by another small outcropping.

The three men ignored the bag, cursing loudly as they dashed by it, trying to overtake the truck as it continued to gather speed.

Josh left the shelter of his tree trunk and started up the hill toward the heiau. He saw Tank and Victor helping Diz to his feet. His ropes had already been cut and his gag removed.

Josh glanced back. The men were still chasing the runaway truck. Josh's eyes fell on the small bag that had fallen from the truck. *Maybe I should pick that up,* he thought. *No, we'd better just get out of here while we can.* He sprinted up the hill and onto the low end of the heiau. "Run toward the back end!" he hissed. "Let's get out of here fast!!"

They ran down the hill until they thought they were safe.

As they caught their breath, Diz explained, "I wanted to return those rocks to the place where I picked them up," he said, puffing with exertion. "I thought I was being very careful, especially when I saw two men down by the truck."

"There were three men," Josh reminded Diz.

"I know that now, but I didn't think of that at the time. The two men had their backs to me, so I climbed up on top of the heiau as quietly as I could."

"What about the third man?" Tank prompted.

"I'm coming to that. I left the rocks on the heiau and started back across, keeping low so the two men by the truck couldn't see me. As

I started down the far back side, I accidentally kicked a loose stone."

"And it made noise and the men came running," Victor guessed.

"No," Diz replied with a shake of his head. "The rock landed on the bald man's head. He was back behind the heiau, so I practically landed on top of him."

Tank chuckled, "That's our Diz!"

"That just made him mad. I ran, but he grabbed me," Diz said, "and he was too strong for me."

"What did they do after they tied you up?" Josh asked.

"They were loading the truck."

"With what?" Josh wanted to know.

"Boxes. That's all I could see, but they apparently had been hidden under the heiau."

Josh asked, "You mean, there's a room or something under there?"

"Must be. But it's so well hidden that none of us saw it."

The boys speculated about what was in the boxes as they began to jog toward Victor's home. They rushed in and excitedly reported to Mrs. Aka what had happened. She promptly called the police. Two officers arrived, questioned the boys, then said they would check out the heiau.

Later the police reported that they had found two men trying to get the panel truck free of some trees where it had crashed. The two men, accused of seizing Diz, told the authorities that the bald-headed man was an ex-convict named Clement Quigley. He had come with another vehicle and carried off the boxes Josh had seen in the back of the truck. A small room under the heiau, well camouflaged, was empty. The two arrested men refused to tell what had been in the boxes, or where their escaped partner might have taken them.

"They obviously were stealing something," Tank said that evening as the four boys walked down the road. "But what?"

None of them had any idea.

There was a full moon that night, so Josh had persuaded the other boys to return to the small beach where they had first seen the mysterious lights. He wanted to see if they would come again.

Instead of taking his ukulele, Victor had brought a portable radio so the boys could listen to music from a Honolulu station. They built a small fire and sat around it, enjoying the music but saying very little.

Josh, Tank, and Disaster Davis were flying back to Honolulu in the morning, so this was their last night together. This time tomorrow night, Diz would be flying across the Pacific on the Red Eye Express.

Finally Diz broke the silence. "You guys are great, and you saved my life. Josh, I'll never forget the risk you took in releasing the brakes on that truck. I owe you big."

"Forget it," Josh replied.

"I can't do that," Diz sighed. "I just wish that I could have returned Kalani's surfboard to her."

Josh put his hand on Diz's shoulder. "I know," he said quietly, and quickly changed the subject because he didn't want the evening to end on a "down" note. "What do you think was in those boxes the bald man got away with?"

"Something mighty valuable, since they were willing to grab Diz and tie him up," Tank answered. "I'm not sure if that's the same as kidnapping, but it's certainly a serious offense. And there's no telling what they would have done to him if we hadn't rescued him."

"I wonder where that bald man is now?" Victor mused.

"Wherever he is," Tank answered, "you can be sure he's mighty unhappy with us."

"Counting Kong, that makes it unanimous," Josh said with an

effort at humor. He looked out to sea where the moon, rising above the mountain behind them, made a shimmering bridge of light on the water.

Josh turned to look up at the mountain. "I don't think those lights are going to show tonight."

"Oh? Why not?" Tank asked.

"Because I think they were a diversion last time—a way to make us and others watch the lights vanish while the crooks moved their stolen goods on or off of this island."

Victor said, "No, those lights will come because they're from the night walkers."

"No such thing as night walkers," Josh replied. "Here, I'll show you." He stood up. "If there were night walkers, they should march right over there to the water with their lights and spears to fish. So I'll just go over and wait."

"Don't!" Victor protested.

"Oh, it's okay," Tank said. "Nothing's going to happen to him."

Victor still protested, but Josh walked along the edge of the water to where there was an area clear of brush leading up the mountain. He heard the music end on the radio.

The announcer said, "I've just been handed a bulletin from our newsroom. Island police today have been asked by Mainland authorities to be on the lookout for millions of dollars' worth of stolen computer chips.

"They were originally taken from a manufacturer's warehouse in Silicon Valley south of San Francisco. Authorities have traced the missing merchandise to Honolulu. It was believed to have been taken from a cargo jet that landed in Honolulu on a refueling stop between California and Asia. Authorities are investigating a lead that there may be a connection between two arrests made on Molokai this afternoon. No details are available, but one suspect escaped and is considered dangerous."

Josh snapped his fingers. "Of course!" he exclaimed aloud. "It all ties together . . . " His voice trailed off when he saw someone on a surfboard paddling along the calm waters offshore. The surfer moved into the bright patch of light made by the moonlight.

Josh frowned. *Who would be surfing at night, even on a nice one like this?*

"Hey!" The surfer stopped paddling and looked toward shore. "Dat you, Waltah?"

Josh recognized Kong's voice. He didn't answer, but little ripples of fear ran down his arms.

"Kong look foh you, yeah?" the surfer said, turning his board toward the beach.

Josh debated about what to do as Kong called again.

"Hey, Waltah! Why you no ansah Kong?"

Josh replied, "I'm not Walter. I'm Josh Ladd."

Kong let out a strangled cry. "Josh Ladd? You wait dehr, haole boy! Kong come teach you good!"

Josh's mind screamed for him to run, but his pride made him stand fast. *Think!* he told himself. *Think! Think! While you're still in one piece!*

Kong waded ashore, carrying the long board. He stuck it in the sand at the edge of the water and started walking purposefully toward Josh.

Josh gulped, still trying to decide what to do.

Suddenly, in the moonlight path on the water, a diver rose up, his black wet suit reflecting a silver sheen. Both Josh and Kong turned to watch him as he stood and waded toward the boys, carrying a spear gun.

He called, "Which one of you is Josh Ladd?"

Kong demanded, "Who wants to know dat?"

"I do," the stranger replied, pulling the hood of his wet suit off so the moonlight reflected on his bald head.

Josh sucked in his breath, recognizing the ex-convict that the police had identified as Quigley.

He looked at Josh. "You're the haole, so that means you're Ladd." Quigley glanced at Kong. "But since you're with him, that makes you equally guilty."

Kong sputtered, "You pupule, mistah!"

Josh asked, "Guilty of what?"

"You know! You got my two friends jailed and cost me ten million dollars! Now, you're going to pay."

He motioned toward the ocean with the spear gun. "Now, move. You're both going for a long moonlight swim!"

Chapter Fifteen

WAITING FOR THE RED EYE

Josh was amazed at how fast a nice evening had exploded into a deadly, life-threatening situation. He protested, "Look here, mister . . ."

"Shut up, kid, and move!" The diver stood aside so the two boys could pass. His movement put him behind the long surfboard which Kong had left sticking up in the sand. It created a shadow over Quigley's face and body.

Kong angrily demanded, "Who you t'ink you . . . ?"

"I said, shut up!" the ex-convict interrupted. He motioned with the sling gun. "Into the water you go."

Josh's mind reeled at the sudden dramatic turn of events. He glanced at Kong, whose belligerent, bullying manner suddenly seemed to have fled. Instead, the moonlight clearly showed fear on his face as he started reluctantly toward the water.

Josh desperately tried again. "Mister, can't you at least tell us why you're angry?" Josh knew the answer, but he was trying to stall while frantically thinking of a way out of this dangerous situation.

"You know why! You've been meddling for days! But when you

released the brakes on our truck loaded with computer chips, that did it!"

Kong asked, "Computah chips?"

Quigley ignored him and kept talking to Josh. "That little trick of yours got my so-called friends caught. I use that term because I got away with all the chips, but my 'friends' plea-bargained,* telling the cops where I'd hidden the chips in exchange for lighter prison sentences. The police seized all thirty million dollars' worth of our chips."

Kong whistled. "Thu'ty million?" he repeated.

"So," Quigley concluded, "I can't get my share back, but I'll feel better if you boys pay for it. Now, stop stalling and get into the water."

Josh's mind raced. *Maybe I can dive underwater and swim away before he can use that thing. But Kong . . . ?*

Josh pointed at the other boy. "He didn't have anything to do with this, so please let him go."

"Nice try," Quigley said sarcastically, "but you're both going with me." He motioned toward the ocean with the sling gun.

If I can just knock that thing down . . . , Josh thought, but didn't finish. He snapped off his thoughts as Disaster Davis called from the shadows under the palm trees.

"What's going on?"

"Go back, Diz!" Josh called through a mouth that was now very dry with fear.

Diz kept coming, stepping into the open where the moon clearly showed his long, gawky frame. "Who are you talking . . . ?"

The diver broke in. "Good! That makes three of you. Step over here with these other two."

Josh watched helplessly while Diz kept coming, his bare feet kicking up little bits of sand in the moonlight.

"What's going on?" Diz repeated innocently, moving toward the ex-convict. Then he smiled. "I get it! You're all playing a game, and I'm supposed to guess what it is, huh?"

Josh groaned inwardly, but he couldn't think of any way to stop Diz from blundering into greater danger.

"You dumb kid!" the diver shouted. He still stood between Josh and Kong in the shadow of the long surfboard standing in the sand. "Stop right there!"

"I know you fellows are only pretending," Diz said, still coming.

Josh tensed, making an instant decision. He thought, *I can't wait any longer!*

With a mighty roar that tore his throat, Josh leaped forward. Using his right arm, he struck down with all his strength at the man's hand holding the spear gun.

At the same time, Diz's long legs covered the last few steps to the surfboard. His gangly arm reached out and shoved hard against the top. The heavy board crashed down, smashing into the side of the diver's head and shoulders. He stumbled and fell to the sand with a moan, the board on top of him.

"Quick, Josh!" Diz yelled, leaping on top of the board and the prostrate man. "Get the spear! Kong, help me sit on him! Tank! Victor! Help us!"

Moments later, Tank, Diz, and Kong were sitting beside Quigley, who lay stretched out on the sand. His wrists had been tied behind him with Victor's belt before the boy ran for home to call the police.

Josh finished checking the ex-convict's head. "He's going to have a headache from that big knot you gave him, Diz," Josh observed, "but I think it's not serious."

Quigley threatened the boys, but they ignored him.

Josh said cheerfully, "I never thought I'd see the time when you three would all be sitting down together."

Kong smiled, his teeth flashing white in the moonlight. "Kong like dis kine set down, yeah."

"I'm sure you do," Josh replied, "but I think you can get up now. Our prisoner isn't going anywhere."

As the four boys stood, Josh smiled and threw his arms around Diz. "You know," Josh exclaimed joyfully, "I don't know whether to laugh or cry. I thought you were really dumb when you kept walking toward him a while ago, but now I realize what you were planning to do. That was a very brave thing."

Diz shrugged. "I came up a few seconds before I said anything. When I saw what was going on, I realized there was only one way to save you and Kong—and the surfboard."

Kong leaned over and picked up the long board from where it lay in the sand beside the prisoner. "Kong not be nice to you," he said softly to Diz. "But you save Kong, yeah?"

"Aw," Diz explained, "I was only practicing the Golden Rule."

"What dat?" Kong asked.

"Doing to others what I would have them do to me," Diz explained.

Kong shook his massive head. "No mattah why, you wahn good malihini. So . . . here." He shoved Kalani's board into Diz's hands. "Dis belong you, yeah?"

"Actually," Diz answered, "it belongs to the father of a girl I know. She'll be glad to know I kept my promise to return it."

* * *

The next morning, Josh, Tank, and Diz flew back to Honolulu

where Mr. Ladd and Detective Penley met them.

After congratulating the boys, Penley told them that all three men involved in the case had been caught and were awaiting trial. Then the detective asked, "Josh, when did you catch on that Quigley was stealing computer chips?"

"Not until he came out of the water. I sure was slow to figure that out. And I still don't know how they stole those chips, and why they were so valuable."

"Well," Penley explained, "there are all kinds of computer chips, worth anything from pennies to thousands of dollars. Those recovered were state-of-the-art chips, each worth $100. They weigh virtually nothing, a quarter to half an ounce each. So a million dollars' worth could be stolen and carried in a suitcase."

Tank asked, "How were they stolen?"

"There typically hasn't been a lot of security at the manufacturing plants," Penley replied, "because electronic thefts are a fairly new kind of crime. Chips are kept in loose cages, so an employee in a stockroom, or someone who knew such a cooperative employee, could steal the chips. Of course, the companies are now being more careful."

Diz asked, "But why did the bald guy have a wet suit?"

"Quigley's friends arranged with a crooked airline employee to steal thirty containers from an airliner that had stopped for refueling in Honolulu. The friends took a boat and dropped the chips off of Molokai in waterproof containers. The chips were already factory sealed, one at a time, in plastic or ceramic packages. So they're rather safe. Quigley then recovered the containers and took them to a little room that had originally been made under the heiau."

"And the lights we saw?" Tank asked.

"A diversionary tactic," the detective replied. "The gang walked down the side of the mountain with flaming torches so that people would become afraid and stay away from where they were hiding their contraband."

"Belief is sure a powerful thing," Josh admitted.

"But I'm glad we all understand now how it was done, and the whole thing is over."

That evening, Mr. Ladd drove everyone to the Honolulu Airport for Disaster Davis to catch the Red Eye jet back to California. His face was barely visible above all the leis that had been slipped over his head by Josh, Mr. Ladd, Tank, Manuel, and Roger.

Josh noticed that Kalani still held a fragrant pikaki* lei across her left arm, but she made no move to present it to the departing visitor.

Tank lightly punched Diz on the shoulder. "Maybe I misjudged you, Diz. I used to think you were the world's biggest klutz. I blamed you for all the things that happened, but this time I noticed that you weren't always at fault. You're really a nice guy."

"Thanks," Diz replied in a barely audible voice.

"Hey, bruddah!" Roger said, lapsing into pidgin English. "You dah bes'! Kong no punch us out when you gone, yeah?"

Mr. Ladd commented, "Don't expect too much from Kong. The leopard can't change his spots, so Kong's never going to stay changed by himself. Only God can really change a person."

Josh said, "Anyway, it all ended well, but it might not have if it hadn't been for Diz using that surfboard to knock the bald man down."

"Oh," Diz replied, "I was just doing what you would have done for me. The Golden Rule, you know."

Kalani spoke for the first time. "Daniel," she said, looking up at Diz with soft brown eyes. "My father returns tomorrow. He will be pleased that Duke Kahanamoku's surfboard is safe."

"It was close," Diz admitted shyly, "and for a while I thought I wasn't going to be able to keep my promise to you about returning it on time."

"But you did," she replied in her musical voice. "My mother says that you are not the same boy who had that accident at church. She says to tell you that she forgives you for ruining my dress."

Diz squirmed and nodded but didn't say anything.

Kalani continued, "Daniel, I can't tell you how much I appreciate all that you did in getting the board back. But at least I can give you this."

She raised the sweet-smelling pikaki lei and eased it over Diz's long skinny neck. Then she gave him a quick kiss on the cheek. "Old Hawaiian custom," she explained, dropping her eyes while the boys made teasing sounds.

When they had quieted down, Diz had an embarrassed look, but his voice was cheerful. "You know what, everybody?" He paused as the public address system announced his flight.

Then he finished, "I liked this trip so much that I hope to return real soon!"

Tank, Roger, and Manuel joined in a loud mock moan.

GLOSSARY

CHAPTER 1:

Aka: (ah-KAH) Hawaiian for "Jacob," or in this case, "Jacobs."

Molokai: (mo-LOH-ky-ee, more commonly called moh-LOH-ky) One of Hawaii's most unchanged islands, it's only 10 miles wide and 37 miles long. Two volcanoes formed the main island before a third volcano created the peninsula of Kalaupapa.

Maui: (MAU-ee) Second largest of the main Hawaiian islands; 728 square miles in area.

Kamakou: (Kah-mah-koe-oo) A 4,970-foot-high mountain which was formed along with the jagged northeast mountains by the second of two major volcanoes that created the island of Molokai.

Ukulele: (oo-ku-LAY-LEE) Commonly mispronounced you-keh-lay-lee, it literally means "leaping flea." It was introduced to the islands by the Portuguese.

138

Menehunes: (meh-nah-HOO-nays) A race of tiny people in Hawaiian legend who are credited with building many temples, fishponds, and roads. They worked only at night, and if their work was not completed in one night, it remained unfinished.

Hoku: (hoe-coo) Hawaiian for "full moon."

Kamaaina: (kham-ah-EYE-nah) An Hawaiian word meaning "child of the land," or "native."

Kapu: (KAH-poo) A warning which means "taboo," " forbidden," or "keep out" in Hawaiian.

Sling gun: A device used for underwater fishing. It employs an elastic band to propel a dart or spear tied to the front of the gun.

Kiawe: (kay-AH-vay) A very thorny algaroba or mesquite tree that grows mostly in dry areas. Kiawe may reach 60 feet in height.

Heiau: (HAY-ow) Temple grounds where the ancient Hawaiians held religious services.

Lanai: (LAH-nye) Hawaiian for a "patio, " "porch, " or "balcony." Also, capitalized, Lanai is a smaller Hawaiian island.

Honolulu: (hoe-no-LOO-LOO) Hawaii's capital and the most populous city in the fiftieth state is located on the island of Oahu. In Hawaiian, Honolulu means "sheltered bay."

CHAPTER 2:

Akamai: (AH-kah-my) Smart, intelligent.

Bruddah: (BRUD-ah) Pidgin English for "brother."

Pidgin English: (PIDJ-uhn) A simplified version of English. It was originally used in the Orient for communication between people who spoke different languages.

Da kine: (dah-kine) Pidgin for "the kind." This is more of an expression and is therefore usually not translated literally.

Cul-de-sac: (KUL-da-sak) A street closed at one end. It's from the French words meaning "bottom of the sack."

Snipe hunt: A prank played on an unsuspecting person who is persuaded by others to go into a wooded area alone with a sack to hunt snipe, a long-billed game bird commonly found in marshy areas. The victim of the trick is instructed to stand motionless, make a certain call, and hold the sack open. The snipe is supposed to walk into the sack, but that never happens. Meanwhile, the other people go off and have a good laugh at the expense of the gullible person.

Oleanders: (OH-lee-an-ders) A poisonous evergreen shrub with white, pink, or red flowers.

Be-still tree: A short, poisonous tree with dense green foliage and bright yellow flowers that fold up at night.

Kamuela: (kam-uh-WAY-la) Hawaiian for "Samuel."

Skeg: A fin on the rear bottom of a surfboard that's used for steering and stability. Modern surfboards often have two or three fins.

Waikiki Beach: (WHY-kee-KEE) Hawaii's most famous white sand beach. Waikiki is Hawaiian for "spouting water."

Makauhine: (mah-kah-oo-HEE-nee) Hawaiian for "mother" or "mama."

Huhu: (HOO-hoo) Angry.

Foh: (foe) Pidgin English meaning "for."

Calabash cousin: (KAL-ah-bash) Any loosely related person, even a close friend. The term arose from the old custom of everyone dipping fingers into a common bowl and sharing a meal.

Bettah: (bet-TAH) Pidgin for "better."

Holo holo: (HOE-lo HOE-lo) More commonly used to mean "go for a walk," but it also means "ride," "sail," etc.

Haole: (HOW-lee) An Hawaiian word originally meaning "stranger," but now used to mean "Caucasians," or "white people."

CHAPTER 3:

Waikiki: (WHY-kee-KEE) The area or district of Honolulu around the famous beach.

Plumeria: (ploo-MARE-y-ah) Also called frangipani (FRAN-gee-PAN-ee) A shrub or small tree which produces large, very fragrant blossoms. They are popular in leis.

Lei: (Lay) Necklaces or garlands of flowers which are given to people on their Hawaiian arrival or departure, and for special occasions, as when someone joins an island church.

Vanda: (vahn-dah, but more commonly, van-dah) A small orchid that grows wild in Hawaii, often in people's yards. These flowers are popular in leis.

Diamond Head: The 760-foot-high extinct volcano at the east end of Honolulu. It's the most prominent Honolulu volcanic landmark.

Muumuu: (MOO-oo-MOO-oo) This word is sometimes mispronounced as moo-moo. It is a colorful loose dress or gown which is frequently worn by women in Hawaii.

Nani wahine: (nah-NEE wah-HEE-nee) Hawaiian for "pretty female."

Hapahaole: (HAH-pah-HOW-lee) Hapa means "half" or "part," so this is a person who's part Caucasian or white, and part non-white, such as Hawaiian.

Haleiwa: (holly-EE-vah) The principal town on the island of Oahu's north shore. In the summer of 1832, the first missionaries to that area, John and Ursula Emerson, built a school there. They called it (in English), House of the Frigate Bird. In Hawaiian: hale (holly = house) ewa (ee-vah = frigate bird).

Pupule: (poo-POO-lay) Insane, crazy.

CHAPTER 4:

Bumby: (BUM-bee) Pidgin for "by and by" or "after a while."

Duke Kahanamoku: (kah-ha-nah-MOE-koo) Hawaiian man who won the 100-meter freestyle swim in two Olympic games. He is best known as the person who popularized surfing.

Polynesian Express: (pol-oh-nee-shun) The slang term for powerful currents that supposedly could sweep someone from Hawaii to the islands as far away as Samoa and Tonga.

Hoolehua: (hoe-oh-lay-hoo-ah) A community on Molokai perhaps best known for the Molokai Airport where inter-island jets land and take off.

Leper: (lep'r) A person afflicted with leprosy, the dreaded disease of the Bible that disfigures and causes loss of fingers, toes, and other extremities. Now called Hansen's disease, it still exists, but is medically treatable. From 1866 to 1946, lepers in Hawaii were forcibly exiled to Kalaupapa. Some patients are still there, but their cases are arrested, so they are free to leave.

Kalaupapa: (kah-lah-PAH-PAH) A very isolated, 4.5-square-mile peninsula on the island of Molokai's north shore. Kalaupapa is surrounded by immense ocean-facing cliffs and fortress-like mountains.

CHAPTER 5:

Lilikoi: (LEE-LEE-coy) Hawaiian for "edible passion fruit."

Leprechaun: (LEP-reh-kon) In Irish folklore, an elf-like little person.

Slippahs: (slip-pahs) The pidgin pronunciation for slippers or thonged sandals commonly worn in the islands.

Lava tubes: (LAH-vuh) A hollow tube made when hot lava flowed across the land. The outside lava hardened first, forming a crust through which the hot interior lava continued to flow. Eventually, most of the lava drained out of the inside, leaving a tunnel or tube.

Monkeypod tree: An ornamental tropical tree that has clusters of flowers, sweet pods eaten by cattle, and wood used for carving.

Aloha spirit: A loving attitude beyond friendliness.

CHAPTER 7:

Malihinis: (mah-lah-HEE-nees) Hawaiian for "newcomers."

Pilikia: (pee-lee-KEE-ah) Hawaiian for "trouble."

Aloha: (ah-LOW-hah) A very practical Hawaiian word with varied meanings, including "hello," "good-bye," and "love." In this chapter, the word means "love."

CHAPTER 9:

Sashimi: (saw-SHE-me) Japanese word for "raw fish," a delicacy in the islands. Only certain very fresh fish are used.

Tofu: (toe-foo) A Japanese bean curd.

Tako: (tah-KOE) A Japanese word for "octopus." The word is also used in Hawaii, which has a large population of Japanese descent.

Oahu: (oh-WAH-hoo) Hawaii's most populous island and the site of its capital city, Honolulu.

Kahuna: (kah-HOO-nah) Anyone (man or woman) expert in any profession. In ancient times, it meant a wizard, priest, etc. In the 1840s, doctors and dentists were called kahunas.

Mauka: (mow-KAH) Hawaiian for "inland," but commonly used for "mountain," because they're inland from the sea.

Royal palm: A tall, graceful palm tree.

Board and batten: A house with a particular style of siding. Wide boards or sheets of lumber are set vertically, and the joints are covered by small strips of wood (battens).

Papaya: (pa-PIE-ah) A large, oblong, yellow fruit common in Hawaii.

CHAPTER 10:

Aloha shirt: (ah-LOW-hah) A loose-fitting man's Hawaiian shirt worn outside the pants. The garment is usually very colorful.

Hibiscus: (hi-BIS-cus) A common Hawaiian plant having a large, open blossom. Although available in many colors, no particular one is designated for this, the state flower.

Bougainvillea: (boo-gun-VEEL-ee-yah) A common tropical ornamental climbing vine with small flowers of many colors, including red, lavender, coral, and white.

CHAPTER 11:

Lahaina: (lah-HIGH-nah) A seaport town of 6,100 on the northwest coast of Maui. Once the whaling capital of the mid-Pacific, it's now a center of tourism, shopping, and pineapple and sugarcane farming.

Maalaea Bay: (ma-ah-LAY-ah bay) An ocean bay on the island of Maui, which is a port for pleasure and fishing boats.

Kahului: (kah-hoo-LOO-ee) A town of 13,000 on the north shore of Maui; the island's main seaport and site of its only jet airport; twin city to Wailuku.

Kaunakakai: (kah-oo-nah-KAH-KYE) The biggest town on Molokai where the inter-island ferry docks. There are no stoplights or shopping centers in the town, and it is only one of three on the island with gas stations.

Kalohi Channel: (kah-loh-hee) The waterway off of Molokai's southwesterly shore separating the northwestern shores of the island of Lanai, which is nine miles away.

Kahoolawe: (kah-hoe-oh-LA-vay) An uninhabited island of 45 square miles located 10 miles southwest of Maui.

Molokini: (moe-low-KEE-nee) An islet that's really the tip of an ancient volcano rising from the ocean floor. The U.S. Coast Guard maintains an unmanned beacon light on this uninhabited speck of land.

CHAPTER 12:

Red Eye: A term for an airliner flying late at night, usually arriving at its destination early the following morning. The expression is believed to have originated because of sleepless flyers arriving with tired, red eyes.

Kamehameha V: (kah-MAY-hah-MAY-hah) The fifth king of Hawaii to be named after the original chief who unified all of the Hawaiian islands and became their first king.

Alii: (ah-LEE-ee) Hawaiian word for native royalty.

Tsunami: (soo-NAH-me) A Japanese word meaning "harbor wave "; it is really a very large sea wave produced by an undersea volcanic eruption or earthquake. The wave rushes into low-lying areas where it does great damage.

Halawa Valley: (hah-la-va) This valley of half a mile wide and four miles deep is protected by high cliffs where Hawaiian tara farmers and fishermen once lived. Jungle growth is now taking over much of the area. There is a scenic view at the top of the narrow road leading up to the cliff tops.

CHAPTER 13:

Pakalolo: (Pah-kah-LO-LO) Hawaiian for "marijuana," an illegal drug made from a plant.

Puhu kauila: (poo-hoo cow-ee-lah) Moray eel, a common tropical, snake-like creature that lives in underwater holes and crevices. These eels can inflict severe wounds with their teeth.

"All things work together for good . . . " is from Romans 8:28.

CHAPTER 15:

Plea-bargained: This is an agreement between a person charged with a crime and the police or the prosecutor that allows the person to plead guilty to a crime less serious than the original crime in exchange for information or help in solving other crimes. The person who plea-bargains gets a reduced punishment.

Pikaki: (pee-KAH-kee) Very fragrant flowers commonly used in leis.

Breakaway

With colorful graphics, hot topics and humor, this magazine for teen guys helps them keep their faith on course *and* gives the latest info on sports, music, celebrities . . . even girls. Best of all, this publication shows teens how they can put their Christian faith into practice and resist peer pressure.

All magazines are published monthly except where otherwise noted. For more information regarding these and other resources, please call Focus on the Family at (719) 531-5181, or write to us at Focus on the Family, Colorado Springs, CO 80995.

Caution! Danger and Surprises Ahead!

Twist your way through a maze of mystery and thrills. Twelve-year-old Josh Ladd always seems to end up in the middle of risky situations, and *you* can join him and his family in each sensational story of the *Ladd Family Adventure* series. Each hard-to-put-down paperback combines non-stop action and intrigue with unforgettable lessons about trusting God.

Eye of the Hurricane
Josh and Tank race against time and a dangerous storm in search of Josh's father.

Terror at Forbidden Falls
Josh and his friends uncover a dangerous plot to detonate a nuclear device in Honolulu.

Peril at Pirate's Point
When Josh and Tank try to get help for Tank's injured father, they're captured by a pair of dangerous smugglers.

Mystery of the Wild Surfer
A young surfer saves Josh from drowning off the coast of Hawaii. But when Josh tries to befriend him, he and his family are threatened by dangerous men.

Secret of the Sunken Sub
A fun-filled fishing trip takes a perilous turn when Josh witnesses the sinking of a Soviet robot submarine and is pursued by Russian spies.

The Dangerous Canoe Race
Josh and his friends are swept into adventure when they are challenged to an outrigger canoe race by a bully who will do anything to win.

Mystery of the Island Jungle
Josh must find the courage to free his friend from a vicious stranger.

The Legend of Fire
Josh attempts to rescue his father from kidnappers and an erupting volcano.

Secret of the Shark Pit
The Ladds brave a life-or-death race for hidden treasure.